KEIRA'S WOLF SA

Pack Law 2

Becca Van

MENAGE EVERLASTING

Siren Publishing, Inc.
www.SirenPublishing.com

A SIREN PUBLISHING BOOK
IMPRINT: Ménage Everlasting

KEIRA'S WOLF SAVIORS

ISBN: 978-1-62241-088-0

First Printing: June 2012

Cover design by Les Byerley

Printed in the U.S.A.

PUBLISHER
Siren Publishing, Inc.
www.SirenPublishing.com

DEDICATION

To all the people who love the concept of werewolves.
This one is for you.

KEIRA'S WOLF SAVIORS

Pack Law 2

BECCA VAN

Chapter One

Keira O'Lachlan was seated in the beat-up bomb she had bought from a used-car salesman two weeks previously, staring at the sign swinging near the door of the Aztec Club, in Aztec, New Mexico. She was so tired her eyes felt sore and gritty. She'd been on the run for over a month now and knew she was at the end of the road. She'd just run out of cash. When she'd fled, she only had the chance to withdraw the daily limit from her bank account, and there was no way she could touch it and withdraw any more now. If she did, then he would know where she was, and she didn't want that.

Keira was twenty-two years old and had been living with her older adopted brother since the day her parents had been murdered when she was sixteen years old. She and her brother had never gotten along, but she would never have thought he would stoop so low. She had tried to remain friends with him, but he had made her life a living hell. David had been on the scene for six years before Keira had surprised her parents with her conception. Her mom and dad had believed they would never have children of their own, and when her mom had found out she was pregnant with Keira, of course they had been over the moon. Or so they had told Keira when they were alive.

They had been gone for six long years, and she still missed them so much.

Keira had fifty bucks to her name. It didn't matter that she had a trust fund left to her by her parents. She couldn't touch it. If she did, she would be in deeper trouble than she already was. She had traded in her late-model sports car for the old bomb she was currently driving.

She didn't want him to be able to find her by running a check of her license plates, so she had ditched the car her parents had bought her for graduation. She had cried a bucket of tears after she had driven away from that car yard. Her heart had ached and still was, after what she'd had to do. And because she had been so scared and desperate to get away and remain hidden, she hadn't argued over the fact the car salesman had given her a straight swap for her car without adding any cash to the deal. She had just wanted to get away. She had even gone to a chain store and bought cheap clothing off the rack, so no one would know she came from money. Now she was in dire straits, too scared to access her bank account and with nowhere to go.

Keira grabbed her purse from the seat of the bomb, took a deep breath, and headed into the Aztec Club. She was hungry, and she was going to spend the last of her money on good food, rather than the junk she had been eating.

Keira pushed open the door and stepped through. The lighting was rather dim, so she stood in the doorway letting her eyes adjust. She then headed over to a small table close to the door and sat down. She could feel eyes on her but tried to ignore them as she perused the menu. After deciding what she'd order, Keira closed the menu and raised her head. She shifted in her seat when she noticed there were mostly males in the club and only a couple of females. She was uncomfortable with all the attention and was just wondering whether she should leave when a large male came to stand in front of her, blocking her view from the rest of the room.

"What can I get you, honey?"

Keira looked up, and up some more, until she met the greenest, most translucent eyes she'd ever seen. She squirmed in her seat when she felt her pussy begin to leak juices out to dampen her panties and her clit begin to throb.

She cleared her throat before she could speak, ordered a Caesar salad with chicken and a black coffee, then watched as the man walked away from her. He was huge. He had black, collar-length hair, wide shoulders which tapered down to slim hips, and a muscular butt. His legs were long, and she could see his muscles rippling beneath his jeans as he walked away from her. She let her eyes wander to his ass and then up his back. He turned his head, and she felt her cheeks heat as he gave her a grin and a wink. She'd been caught out ogling his butt.

Keira lowered her eyes to the table and fiddled with the menu. She felt so uncomfortable and out of place here, but she didn't know what to do. She wondered if the club needed any extra waitstaff, and she planned to find out before she left. She needed money and a place to stay. She had been living in her car since the moment she had left her hometown of Seattle, Washington, and hadn't looked back since.

Keira shifted in her seat again. She could still feel them all watching her, and since she had never been on her own, except for the last month, she was scared out of her wits. She wanted to grab her purse from beside her and run. Her nerves were stretched so tight she wondered how she was still functioning. She reached for her purse and was about to leave. She slid to the edge of her seat in preparation to rise to her feet, but she froze as her denim-clad knees collided with a pair of muscular legs.

"Are you all right, honey? Did you need something else?"

"No. I'm good," Keira said and made the mistake of cricking her neck to look up into the man's face. He was so sexy that she felt her pussy throb.

"Here you go. Enjoy your meal," the man said as he placed her food and coffee on the table.

"Um, I was wondering if you need any staff. I haven't worked in a place like this before, but I can cook or wait tables," Keira stated hopefully.

The man sat down opposite her in the small booth and studied her. She felt his eyes slide over her body and knew she was blushing again. She had always been quick to blush, and the heat in her cheeks let her know whenever she did. She cursed her pale skin and fair coloring. She hated that she was so shy and nervous around strangers.

"What's your name, honey?"

"K–Karen," Keira replied. "Karen Jones."

"My name is Jake Domain. Pleased to meet you, Karen," Jake said and extended a hand in greeting.

Keira took his hand and pulled back quickly when she felt warmth tingle up the length of her arm. She felt her breasts swell and her nipples pucker and wondered what the hell had gotten into her. She'd never reacted like that to a man before, and she wasn't sure she liked it.

"Why don't you eat your food, and we'll discuss what sort of work you can do," Jake said.

Keira nodded and picked up her fork. Once she began eating, her hunger took over, and she didn't stop to talk until she'd finished the last mouthful. She looked up and smiled sheepishly at the man sitting across from her.

"Sorry, I guess I was hungrier than I thought."

"Don't worry about it, honey. Now that you're done, why don't we get down to business," Jake stated. "Where are you from, Karen?"

"Washington State."

"What are you doing in New Mexico?"

"Uh, I just wanted to explore the country," Keira replied, not meeting Jake's eyes as she lied to him.

"What did you do before you came here?" Jake asked.

"Does it really matter?" Keira asked, because she couldn't think of any answer other than the truth.

She watched as he leaned back in his seat, his arms folding across his wide chest as he studied her. Keira felt like a bug under a microscope. He was looking at her through narrowed eyes, and she could have sworn she saw his eyes glow. She blinked and looked again. No, they weren't glowing. *I'm just letting my imagination run away with me.* Keira sipped the last of her coffee and placed the empty cup back on the table. Jake was making her feel uncomfortable, and she didn't know where to look. He didn't seem to have any trouble. He just kept right on staring at her.

"Do I have lettuce stuck in my teeth or food on my face?" Keira asked irritably.

She watched as Jake smiled at her. Creases formed near the corners of his eyes, and he had sexy dimples showing at the corners of his mouth. God, he was hot. He was at least six foot three of pure, hard muscle. His biceps bulged, and she had to urge to reach out and run her fingertips over his skin. She wondered what his sinewy muscles would feel like beneath her hands. Keira shook her head and blinked. She couldn't believe where her mind was wandering. She'd never had this sort of trouble before.

"If I'm going to hire you, I'd like to know what your skills are," Jake replied.

Keira looked down at the table and fiddled with her cup. She was so nervous and horny, she couldn't stop fidgeting.

"I'm a bookkeeper," Keira replied, giving a half truth. In fact, she was a fully qualified accountant, but for some reason she didn't want him knowing that. Then she realized why. If he had the notion to check on her and ran the false name she'd just given him, he would know she had been deceitful from the start.

"Are you in trouble? Do you have the law after you?" Jake asked.

Keira looked up at that question and answered him honestly. "No. I don't have the law looking for me."

"Do you want a refill, honey?" Jake asked, pointing to her empty coffee mug.

"Please," Keira answered.

"Devon, bring the coffeepot," Jake called.

Keira noticed the man behind the bar reach for a coffeepot and disappear out the side door, and then he was striding toward her table. He was just as handsome as Jake, but he was even bigger. His hair was a dark brown, and his eyes were hazel. He filled her cup and just stood staring down at her.

"Devon, this is Karen Jones. Karen, this is my brother, Devon," Jake introduced.

Keira shook the proffered hand and flinched as the warmth of his skin sent tingles up her spine. She felt goose bumps break out and pulled her hand back quickly. *What the fuck, Keira? Stop being such a slut. How can I be attracted to two men at the same time?*

"I'm pleased to meet you, Devon," Keira squeaked out as she lowered her eyes. She heard a low rumbling sound and looked back up at Devon. She could have sworn she saw his eyes glow for a minute. *Get a hold of yourself, girl. You're going crazy.*

"The pleasure's all mine, sweetheart," Devon replied.

Keira jumped when Devon placed a hand on her shoulder and nudged her over. She slid into the corner of the small booth and watched as Devon sat down beside her. She felt nervous energy travel through her body and wondered if she was about to snap.

"So, what are you two talking about?" Devon asked.

Keira couldn't prevent her body shuddering in reaction to the deep, gravelly voice which seemed to flow over her and go straight down to her pussy. She crossed her legs and squeezed her thighs together, trying to ease the ache in her cunt.

"Karen was asking about a job. She's says she'd do anything, but she was a bookkeeper in Washington," Jake answered his brother.

Keira jumped when she the door nearby crashed open. She turned her head, and her eyes met the brown ones staring at her, and then she looked at the two Domain brothers. She turned back again and studied the new man. He had similar features to Jake and Devon, and she wondered if he was their brother. He had to be at least six foot six, and he literally bulged with muscles. He pinned her to her seat with his heated stare. She lowered her eyes to the table, picked up her coffee with two hands, hoping the shake in them wasn't visible, and sipped the dark brew. She didn't need to look up to know he was standing over their table. He pushed Jake and sat down in the booth. Keira felt so crowded and claustrophobic. She felt her heart give a thump in her chest, and her breathing escalated. She could feel the new arrival's eyes on her but was too afraid to look up.

"Karen, this is our oldest brother, Greg. Greg, this is Karen Jones," Jake introduced.

Keira peeked at him and gasped as he pinned her with his eyes. His eyes were glowing as he stared at her, and even though she wanted to look away, she couldn't seem to manage the task. Her brain was fried.

She watched as Greg reached across the table and took her hand in his. Her hand looked so small and pale engulfed in his massive fingers. She tried to pull away, but he wouldn't allow it. She looked up again and felt herself drowning in the depths of his now-glowing amber eyes.

"Pleased to meet you, Karen. I hear you're looking for work," Greg said.

Keira wondered how the hell he knew that. He had only just arrived, so he hadn't heard the conversation she'd had with his brother.

"Yes," Keira squeaked then cleared her throat. "Yes, I am looking for work."

"It just so happens we need a bookkeeper for the club. You're hired, honey. We can even let you stay in one of the rooms upstairs. Where's your car? I'll help you get your stuff," Jake said as Greg stood up.

"Out the front," Keira replied. "Thank you for giving me a chance. I won't let you down."

"We know you won't, baby. Come on, we'll all help unload and get you settled in," Greg stated.

Keira wondered what was with all the endearments. She'd never had anyone call her such things, except for her parents. She was wary of these three men. They seemed too eager to want her around. But her libido was overriding her brain, and she was just too damn curious and turned on to say anything just now.

Keira sighed as Devon moved from the seat and reached for her hand. He helped her to her feet, but when she tugged to get her hand free he wouldn't let go. She wondered if she was jumping from the frying pan into the fire.

Chapter Two

Jake and his brothers helped get Karen's stuff from her car. He and his wolf had smelled her as soon as she walked through the door. His wolf had prowled beneath his skin, frustrated and anxious to claim her. He'd pushed his beast back down and studied her from behind the bar. She was so small and petite compared to him. Her shoulder-length hair was blonde, streaked through with red and brown highlights. He'd let his eyes rove over her body. He'd paused on the soft mounds of her lush breasts, and his cock had hardened even more. She couldn't be any taller than five foot five, and she had nice, rounded hips and long, slim legs. She came from money. He could see that by the way she moved and acted. He wondered if she was a runaway. She had the sweetest eyes he'd ever seen. They were a combination of green and blue. He'd inhaled deeply and smelled her fear. He'd wanted to jump the bar and wrap her in his arms. He'd looked at his younger brother Devon and known he was battling his own beast as he stared at the beautiful woman.

Jake had watched as she clutched her purse to her chest. She'd looked ready to bolt back out the door. She'd straightened her shoulders and walked over to the closest booth. She'd sat down but slid around the curved seat a little so her back was to the window. He'd watched her reach for a menu and hide her face behind it. Jake couldn't stand being so far away from her. He'd wanted to sniff her and roll in her scent, but had settled for going over to her to take her order. She'd looked up at him, and he'd seen her eyes widen, and then she had been staring. *Good.* It seemed his mate wasn't immune to him either. He'd taken her order and sent Devon out back to get Mac to prepare her meal. He'd known it wouldn't be long before he would be back by her side. His wolf had been butting against him, pushing him to stake his claim.

Jake had placed her order on the table and tried to think of something to ask her, to stay by her side, but she had surprised him by beating him to it. She'd asked if he had any work available, and he'd had to stop himself from rubbing his hands together. She'd just given him a reason to stay, and he wasn't about to pass it up.

Jake had talked with her, introducing himself, and knew she was lying about her name as she hesitated when giving it. He could still smell her fear and nervousness and wanted to pick her up, to hold her tight. Devon had brought the coffeepot over when he asked, and he'd watched as Karen jumped when his brother placed a hand on her shoulder to nudge her over. His brother had sat beside their mate and he'd heard him growl low in his chest. Jake had glared at Devon, letting him know to get a hold of his beast so he wouldn't scare their mate away.

Jake had known Devon had contacted their older brother Greg telepathically and knew his brother was on his way to the club. He'd wondered how their little mate would react to meeting his much-larger-built and taller brother. He didn't have long to wait. Just as that thought had popped into his head, his brother had come crashing through the club doors.

Jake could smell Karen's desire for them and wanted to pick her up, lay her over the bar, and sink his cock into her pussy, but he knew that wasn't about to happen. Their little woman was so skittish she couldn't sit still. He'd watched her pupils dilate as she'd looked up into Greg's eyes. He'd seen her shiver and known she was turned on by all three of them. He'd hired her on the spot, and then he and his brothers had walked outside to help her unload her car.

"Which is your car, honey?" Jake now asked, already eyeing the piece of rusted-out junk close to the club's doors. He could smell her scent on the car and knew it was hers. He wanted to get it towed and replace it with a new car, but knew he didn't have the right. Not yet, at least. But if he had his way, she wouldn't be driving that piece of junk ever again. Her actions and grace belied the car she drove and the cheap clothes she wore. He wondered whom and what she was running from. He moved in close to Karen as she unlocked the door to her car. He could see at a glance she had been living in the vehicle. What he wanted to know was for how long. He gently moved her to the side, reached in, and unlocked the back door. He and his brothers began unloading her stuff. She only had one bag of clothes that he could see, and he wondered how long she been running. There was a quilt in the backseat and a pillow. Her scent surrounded him as he began to gather up her stuff.

"Follow me, honey. My brothers can get the rest of your stuff. Let me show you to your room," Jake said and walked to the side of the club.

He led her up a set of stairs and through the door. He walked to the first door off the hallway and stepped into the room. It wasn't much, but it was clean and comfortable. He placed Karen's stuff on the queen-size bed and turned to see her standing in the doorway. She jumped when she heard Devon and Greg coming up behind her. She moved farther into the room, just off the doorway, so his brothers could get through the entrance.

"Is there any more?" Jake asked his brothers.

Jake looked at the pitiful amount of stuff she had but gave a negligible shrug since he could do nothing about it, *yet*. He walked toward Karen and watched as she stood up straight as if she were about to take him on, and then he saw her cringe and step back. Her back bumped into the wall behind her.

"Take it easy, honey. We're happy to have you on board. I hate doing the figures for the club. You have just taken a load off my shoulders," Jake stated and stopped a few feet from her. "Now, let's get down to business. You start work at ten a.m. There isn't much happening around here before then. You can work through to six. All meals are provided, and so is your room. You'll get a weekly wage on top of that. The pay's not much to start with, but you will have a three-month probationary period just like everyone else. If you don't like something, you will come to one of us and talk about it. If you have *any* problems at all, again, come to one of us and we'll help you. Do you have any questions?"

"No. Thank you for helping me unload and for giving me a job. You don't know how much I appreciate it," Karen stated.

Jake smiled. She'd really tried to look at each of them in the eye when she'd said that, but she was so shy she ended up looking at her feet again. He slowly reached out and cupped her cheek in his hand and brought her eyes up to his.

"No problem, honey. You look beat. Why don't you have an early night? Oh, one more thing. The bathroom is the second door on the right. Sorry you don't have one off your room, but since no one else is staying here, it's all yours anyway."

"Thanks."

"See you in the morning, baby," Greg said.

"Bye, sweetheart," Devon stated.

"I'll be downstairs until midnight. Just holler if you want anything. Okay?" Jake said and was satisfied when she nodded.

Jake followed his brothers to the end of the hall and down the narrow stairs to the club below. He knew as soon as he was back behind the bar the questions would begin. He only wished he was able to answer them. He still thought she was lying about her name and a lot of other stuff as well. She'd been nervous and evasive when she'd answered his questions. But underneath all that fear and anxiety he could smell her sweet pussy creaming for him. Her musky scent had gotten stronger and stronger with the arrival of his brothers. He was going to have to put word out and about amongst the pack that she was theirs. He'd seen some of the younger Omegas from his pack, the Friess Pack, giving Karen the once-over. He intended to stop that tonight.

Jake stepped up behind the bar with Devon. Greg had already settled himself on a seat at the other side. His older brother stared at him expectantly, and he sighed, knowing he wasn't going to satisfy his brothers' curiosity. He knew that because he was just as frustrated as they were. He wanted to know everything about the woman calling herself Karen. He wanted to know her life story from the moment she was born.

"Where's she from?" Greg asked.

"She says from Washington State," Jake replied.

"You don't believe her?" Greg asked with a frown.

"Actually, I think that was one of the only times she didn't lie. Well, that and about her being a bookkeeper, but she was still hesitant when answering the question of her previous employment. So, who knows?" Jake replied with a shrug.

"Do you think her name is Karen Jones?" Greg asked.

"No."

"Well, fuck. What the hell is she up to?" Greg spat out.

"That I don't know. All I can tell you is she says she's not on the run from the law and I think I believe her on that, at least. She's definitely on the run from something or someone. She's scared shitless," Jake stated needlessly, knowing his two werewolf brothers would have smelled her fear like he had.

"We need to find out who she is. Devon, when she comes down here tomorrow for her shift, I want you to search her room," Greg commanded.

"Don't you think we should give her a chance to come clean first?" Jake asked, frowning at his brother.

"No. I want to know what's going on with our mate. If she's in trouble and needs protecting I want to know about it as soon as possible. We can't protect her if we don't know what we're protecting her from," Greg stated.

"Shit. The last thing we want is to have her running," Jake said. "Are you going to dress down the Omegas that were staring at our mate, or do you want me to?"

"I'll do it," Greg replied.

Jake heard the low, growling rumble in his brother's chest. It was so full of authority even the hackles on the back of his neck stood up on end. His brother talked really low, and he knew none of the humans in the room would be able to hear him. He heard Greg in his head as his brother used the common telepathic link to warn the Omegas.

"The woman calling herself Karen Jones is off-limits to all of you. She's ours. If I catch anyone looking at her or treating her with anything other than respect, you will answer to me and my brothers. Do I make myself clear?"

"Yes, Greg," the Omegas replied, and Jake sighed with relief. He had thought he was going to have to knock a few heads together after the way they had been staring at his mate. He was glad the younger men had decided to listen to his brother's dictate.

"I'm heading back to the den. I intend to clear my calendar and get some of the other Betas to step up and take over until we have our mate safely in our wing of the pack's mansion. I should be back around ten in the morning," Greg told Jake, then left.

"She's fucking gorgeous, isn't she, Jake?" Devon asked him. "My dick stood straight up as soon as she walked in the door."

"Yeah, mine, too. We're going to have to be careful with her until we find out what she's hiding. Don't go pushing her too hard, too fast," Jake stated.

"I won't. There is no way in hell I'm letting her walk away though," Devon said.

Jake sighed as he worked the bar automatically. His thoughts were both on the beautiful woman upstairs and in his pants for the rest of the night.

Chapter Three

Keira stood staring at the bank statement in her hand. A large sum of money had been withdrawn from her account, and she knew it hadn't been her doing. Who the hell had access to her trust fund? The answer flashed before her mind, but she just couldn't comprehend her own brother stealing from her. She knew David had resented her from a very young age, and no matter how hard she'd tried to be his friend, he just kept pushing her away.

She couldn't understand why he was stealing money from her. He was the only one who had access to her account, but she knew he had his own trust fund. Their parents had set up a fund for each of them, and there was more than enough money from the estate for anything they would ever need without ever having to touch their own money. She was going to find David and ask him why he had taken her money.

Keira moved through the house. It felt so empty and still without her parents here. They had been gone for nearly six years, and she still couldn't get used to them not being around. She walked along the thick-carpeted hallway heading for David's office. She loved the feel of the plush pile beneath her bare feet. She often walked around the house with no shoes or socks on. She stopped outside David's office and raised her hand to knock on the door. She stopped her fist from connecting with the wood just in time. The door was slightly ajar, and she heard David talking on the phone to someone. He'd mentioned her name.

"Nah, Keira's a dumb little bitch. She has no idea I've been using the estate money. No, I'll deal with her. Besides, she doesn't trust

easily and she trusts me. She's always trying to be nice and friendly to her only brother. I'll have her out of the picture by the end of the week just like I did with our parents all those years ago."

Keira didn't hang around to hear the rest of the conversation. She rushed up to her bedroom, flung some clothes into a bag, grabbed a spare quilt and pillow, and took off. She stopped at the closest ATM, withdrew the daily limit, and didn't look back.

Keira woke herself up whimpering and sobbing. It had been the same night after night since she had left her home in Seattle. She was shaking and sweating from the aftereffects of her nightmare, and she was so tired. She knew she wouldn't be able to fall asleep again, so she turned on the bedside lamp, propped herself up on the pillows, and stared at the walls and ceiling. She'd come a long way from home and didn't know what to do about her brother. She'd thought about going to the police and reporting him, but she had no idea what he was up to. He could be running drugs or weapons. All she knew was the brother she had worshipped wasn't the man she'd thought he was. She didn't think she could deal with the reality of sending her brother to jail, but she didn't know what else to do. She pulled her legs up close to her body and rested her head on her knees. She'd been surviving on little sleep and knew it was catching up with her. She wanted nothing more than to roll over and sleep for a week, but she knew that wouldn't happen.

By the time the sun began to lighten the sky, Keira was exhausted. Her eyes began to droop, and her body was aching from staying in one position for so long. She eased her legs down the bed and leaned back on the pillows. She would just rest for a moment, and then she would get up and get ready for her first day on the job. Her eyelids closed, and she went to sleep.

Keira jerked upright at the sound of her door opening. *Shit.* He'd found her. She was out of bed and across the room before her eyes were functioning. She had the bedside lamp in her hand but didn't remember picking it up. She must have ripped the cord from the socket because the cord was dangling down and brushing against her leg. Her bleary eyes finally began to focus, and she stood staring at the three large Domain brothers.

"Are you all right, Karen?" Greg asked as he walked toward her. He gently took the lamp from her hand and put it back on the bedside table.

"Yes," Keira squeaked, then paused to clear her throat. "Yes, I'm fine."

"Are you sure, honey?" Jake asked.

"Yes. What are you doing here?" Keira asked the three men as they stared at her body. She could see the heat in their eyes and finally realized she was standing in front of them in nothing but her panties and a T-shirt. She crossed her arms over her breasts to hide the fact she was reacting to their presence. Her areolas prickled, and the skin puckered. Her nipples elongated, becoming two hard points.

"We came to check up on you when you didn't come down to work. We were worried about you, baby," Greg said and moved in closer to her. She saw his nostrils flare as he breathed deeply, and she could have sworn she saw his eyes flash.

Keira blinked as she stared at Greg, and then comprehension dawned. "What time is it?"

"Twenty after ten, honey," Jake answered.

"Shit. I'm so sorry. I can't believe I fell asleep again. If you leave I'll get ready and be down in ten minutes."

"Are you sure you're okay, sweetheart?" Devon asked.

"Yes, thanks, I'm fine."

"Okay, we'll see you in a few, baby. Don't rush, there's nothing that important you have to do today," Greg stated.

Keira watched as the three hot, sexy men left her room. When they were gone she scurried around the room getting her clothes and toiletries and headed for the bathroom. She was in and out of the shower in two minutes flat. She dressed and was downstairs before her ten minutes had passed. She hesitated in the doorway of the narrow stairwell and was glad when Jake appeared. She had no idea where she was supposed to meet him and his brothers. He had just saved her from searching him out.

"This way, honey," Jake said and took her hand in his.

God, what is it about these men that has my libido revving? She let Jake lead her down a hallway and into the kitchen of the club. There were several people already at work in the kitchen. The smell of freshly brewed coffee had her eyes searching for it. She spied a large pot warming on the counter.

Jake led her into the kitchen and introduced her to the other staff. Once that was done he grabbed a couple of mugs from a cupboard and held one up, silently questioning. At her nod of acceptance he poured the dark brew into the mugs and led her out of the kitchen. The club was bigger than it looked from the outside. He led her into a large room containing two desks and a sofa.

"Okay, let me show you how our software works, and I can leave you to it," Jake stated.

Keira glanced toward Devon, who was sitting at the other desk, and Greg, who was sitting on the small sofa. He was so big he took up more than half of the two seats with his wide shoulders. She let Jake seat her at the desk, and then he pulled another chair up next to her. She felt him looking at her, but she kept her eyes on the computer monitor. He showed her the software and how they dealt with all the invoices and purchase orders. He took her through every aspect of the business, and she was impressed by how organized they were. She saw Devon leave the room from the corner of her eye, but didn't think anything of it. He obviously had other things to do. She did wonder what Greg did though. He sat staring at her the whole time Jake was explaining things.

"Thanks, Jake. I think I have it now. It all looks pretty straightforward," Keira said as Jake stood.

"I have a few things I need to be checking on. If you need me for anything, just come find me," Jake said.

Keira sighed with relief when Jake left the room, Greg following behind. She had never been stared at like the way Greg did. It made her feel a little uncomfortable and uncertain. She pushed her thoughts aside, picked up the stack of invoices, and got down to work.

* * * *

Devon met his brothers in one of the storage rooms off the side of the bar. He had called them telepathically. He had taken the opportunity of searching their mate's room while she was busy with Jake. He had made sure not to move anything, and if he did, he put it back where it had been. She had so little clothing it broke his heart. He wondered how long she had been on the run. He was going to get to the bottom of this as soon as he informed his brothers what he had found out.

"Our mate's real name is Keira O'Lachlan. She is from Seattle, Washington. From her address I'd have to say she's from money. A lot of money, but I need to run a check on her, before I can say for certain."

"Why don't you go use the computer in the office where you can keep an eye on her?" Greg asked. "I'm going to contact our Alphas, Jonah, Mikhail, and Brock Friess, and see if I can use Chris to dig up anything he can on our little mate. I know he can find out things we would never be able to," Greg stated.

"Okay, let me know if you two find out anything," Jake said. "I have to go check on the orders that have just arrived."

Devon left the storage room, his brothers on his heels as they all went to do their respective tasks. Devon hesitated in the doorway of the office and leaned against the doorjamb. He watched his little mate working at the computer, her brow furrowed with concentration. He saw the tip of her tongue peek out of her mouth and had to stifle a groan as his cock hardened. He could just see Keira down on her knees in front of him, her sweet lips wrapped around his hard shaft as she licked the head of his dick with that pink little tongue.

She looked up and smiled at him, her eyes still glazed from concentration. He saw her eyes run the length of his body, and they caught on his distended cock pushing against the zipper of his jeans. He smiled wider when red tinged her cheeks and she hurriedly looked away. Her eyes were now glued to the computer monitor, and he wanted to go over to her pick her up and wrap her in his arms. Instead, he walked into the room and sat at the desk a few feet away from her. He could smell the juices leaking from her pussy and had to restrain himself from laying her over his desk and burying his cock into her wet little cunt. Devon got down to work. He needed to know what was going on with his mate.

Chapter Four

"Jake, Devon, we need to meet up away from prying ears and eyes. Meet me out back," Greg commanded his brothers using their telepathic link. He needed to tell his brothers what he had found on their mate.

Greg couldn't believe what Chris Friess, his Alphas' cousin and Beta, had found out about his little mate's adopted brother. David O'Lachlan was involved in a large prostitution ring. He and his cronies kidnapped helpless, innocent young women off the streets and sold them into sexual slavery. He was making millions of dollars supplying underworld mobsters with prostitutes and stealing money from Keira to help fund his exploits. Her brother was gambling heavily and had already gone through the estate trust fund as well as his own trust. He made bets of up to a million dollars at a time and needed his sister's money for his gambling addiction.

The fact the women were being abducted made his blood boil. David was even suspected in the accidental death of Keira's parents, but no solid evidence had been found, so the law hadn't been able to touch the bastard. Keira was such a sweet little innocent and loved her brother even though he treated her like shit. Her brother had even stolen money from Keira's trust account.

Their little Keira obviously knew something or had found out about David's nefarious activities and bolted. Greg was so frustrated at her for not coming clean with them, but he knew he really didn't have a say in her life, as yet. They'd only met her yesterday. He didn't want her staying in the room above the club by herself anymore. He needed to feel that he could protect her. He and his brothers were going to have to figure out a way to get her into their home and bed. She was going to pitch a fit if he demanded she come back to the den with them. Maybe he and his brothers could stay over at the club on a rotational basis. But then she was going to wonder why they weren't going home. Either way she was going to be suspicious. He needed to talk to his brothers so they could figure out what to do to keep their mate safe.

Greg stood outside, breathing in the scents around him. He couldn't smell anything out of the ordinary, and he trusted his wolf senses, so he relaxed, waiting for his brothers. The back door to the club opened, his brothers moving toward him.

"What did you find out?" Jake asked.

"She's on the run, all right," Greg said and explained her brother's nefarious business.

"Fuck. Is the law aware of what he's doing?" Jake asked.

"They have their suspicions, but they haven't been able to get any evidence," Greg replied.

"What made Keira run?" Devon asked.

"I'm not sure. She obviously knows something, otherwise she wouldn't be here. Chris found out David stole money from Keira's trust account. Maybe the missing money put her on alert, or maybe she overheard something," Greg replied. "Her brother is also a suspect in her parents' 'accidental death' six years ago. Again, there was no evidence."

"Fuck it. We have to claim her, Greg. My wolf is pushing hard and so is my dick," Devon stated.

"We can't just walk up to her and tell her we are werewolves and she is our mate. For one, she wouldn't believe us, and secondly, she'd run," Greg said.

"Then what the hell do we do?" Jake asked.

"That's the million-dollar question, isn't it? I don't want her staying here by herself anymore. We need to get her to the den where she'll be safe. What I don't know is how to get her there without making her suspicious," Greg stated.

"What if we tell the truth? We tell her we don't like her staying here by herself. We tell her it's not safe for her to be alone and we want to make sure she is comfortable. We can offer her the spare room in our suite at the mansion," Devon said.

Greg thought about that, pacing back and forth. He turned to his younger brother with a smile. "Good idea. Once we get her in our suite of rooms we start wooing our mate into our bed and our hearts."

Greg and his two brothers entered the club again. Jake left to man the bar. Greg went to the kitchen to grab some food for their little mate. She hadn't even taken time to have breakfast that morning, and since it was just after two in the afternoon he knew she had to be hungry. There was always a supply of sandwiches in the fridge ready for any of the employees to have on their breaks. Greg reached for one of the large platters and grabbed a couple of bottles of water. He was going to let her get away with thinking she had pulled the wool over their eyes with her name for the time being, but once she was in their house, all bets were off.

Greg took the food and water into the office. He found Keira still sitting at the desk entering in the data necessary to run the club. She looked up at him and smiled absently then continued working.

"It's time for a break, baby girl. You haven't stopped since this morning, and I'll bet you're hungry," Greg stated, placing the platter of sandwiches and bottled water on Devon's desk.

"Yes, actually I am rather hungry," Keira replied.

Greg passed her the platter, and she took half a sandwich and bit into it. She groaned with enjoyment, and he felt his cock throb. This was getting to be too much for him and his wolf to take. They had to claim her soon, or his and his brothers' wolves were going to take over. They sat in companionable silence and ate their lunch. Greg smelled Devon approaching the office, and by the rumble he heard coming from his brother's stomach, he was looking for food, too.

"Hi, sweetheart, how's the work going?" Devon asked.

Greg watched Keira interacting and conversing with his brother. She was such a shy little thing, but when she talked about her work, her whole face lit up. He could see her passion as she waved her hands around explaining what she had done. He knew then she wasn't as introverted as she made out. There was passion beneath that shy façade that just hadn't been tapped into yet. He couldn't wait to get their hot little mate into their bed, but first they had to tell her they were werewolves. He wondered how she was going to react. Would she laugh and think they were nuts? Or would she run from the house screaming? He certainly hoped not.

"I have to head back to the house and get some work done. Jonah, my cousin and boss, along with his brothers, runs a large corporation from their home. Apparently they can't do without me," Greg said.

He saw her looking at him. Her eyes glazed over, her pupils dilated, her breathing escalated, and she licked her lips. She leaned toward him, and he took advantage of her arousal. He moved over to Keira, cupped her chin in his hand, and leaned down to brush his lips over hers. He saw the shock in her eyes at his gesture, but he also smelled her desire. Her eyes dilated even more, her heartbeat notched up, and she was breathing heavily. Yep, his little mate wasn't as immune to him and his brothers as she tried to make out.

"I'll see you later, baby," Greg said and headed toward the door. He glanced back when he felt her eyes on him, and couldn't help but grin when he caught her ogling his ass. He left the room without a backward glance.

* * * *

Greg walked into his Alpha and cousin's large office in the back of the den house. He waited until Jonah was off the phone and sat down in the large armchair across from his cousin.

"Fill me in with what's going on with your mate, Greg," Jonah commanded.

Greg spent the next half an hour going over everything he, his cousin Chris, and his brothers had found out about his mate. His Alpha leaned back in his chair and crossed his arms over his chest.

"You need to get her here. She'll be safer at the pack house. Have you spoken to Mikhail or Brock yet?" Jonah asked.

"No. I wanted to talk to you first. I was going to ask to bring Keira here, but you saved me the trouble. We're going to have to beef up security. I don't want Michelle in any danger, either," Greg stated. The last thing Greg wanted was to have Jonah and his brothers, Mikhail and Brock, angry with him for putting their mate, Michelle, in jeopardy.

"I'll get Chris, Blayk, and James on it," said Jonah, and then he heard Jonah use the common mental link to speak with his cousins.

"Chris, I need to see you and your brothers in my office as soon as possible. We need to discuss a few things."

"We'll be there in fifteen minutes, Alpha," Chris replied.

"I can't believe she was living with a murderer for the last six years. God, he could have taken her out at any time, and we would never have met her," Greg said, running a hand through his hair with frustration.

"That's your wolf talking, Greg. You are going to have to claim her as soon as you can. I can feel your wolf pacing. Have you told her about us yet?"

"No. I'm just a tad worried how she'll react. I was planning on telling her tonight when we bring her here. Do you think Michelle will be able to help her if she gets all hysterical? Fuck, I'm scared if she runs my wolf is going to take over, and then where will we be? The last thing I want to do is have her running from my wolf in terror."

"You and your brothers work on getting her here. I'll let the pack know to keep the animal tendencies to a minimum until you've told your mate what we are. There is a pack run planned for tonight. I think you and your brothers should attend. Maybe letting off a bit of steam will help control your wolves," Jonah advised.

"You're probably right," Greg said with a sigh.

"I'll have Michelle keep Keira company, but as soon as you get her in the door, I want you to let her know you know what's going on. Someone will slip up and call her by her real name, and then the shit really will hit the fan," Jonah stated.

Chris, Blayk, and James entered the office and sat down. Greg and Jonah explained the situation with Keira, and his cousins immediately got to work at their desks on the other side of the room. Greg and Jonah were chatting about the pack members and what they needed to do to keep the women safe when Chris spoke.

"We are going to need to be more vigilant protecting the women. Your mate's brother is on her trail. He has found where she traded her car for the other. She's been careful but forgot about the transfer papers when she traded her vehicle. It's only a matter of time before he finds her," Chris said.

"How the hell did you find that out so quickly?" Jonah asked.

"We have specialized software. I typed in your mate's name, and any information on her, whether provided by her or not, sends back an alert," Chris explained.

"Okay. Well, that's good. I'm not even going to ask where you got that program. I don't think I want to know. Make sure all the males in the pack are on full alert," Greg commanded. "We have an obligation to make sure our women are kept safe."

Chapter Five

Keira had finished up work for the day. She had made sure to work late to make up for her tardiness that morning. She saved the program she had been working on then shut down the computer. She was looking forward to a nice, hot shower, and then maybe she would head down to the bar for a drink. She headed for the shower. She undressed and turned the faucets on. Nothing happened. What the hell? She fiddled with taps, turning them on and off a few times, but still nothing. She tried the faucets at the sink and got the same results. She gave a frustrated sigh, re-dressed sans underwear, and headed downstairs.

Keira sat on a barstool and waited for Jake to finish serving a customer. She watched the easy grace with which he moved. The muscles in his arms and abs rippled, making her squirm in her seat.

"Hey, honey, do you want a drink?"

"No, well, maybe. I was going to have a shower then come down for a drink but the shower isn't working. There's no water at all in the upstairs bathroom," Keira stated.

"What? Well, shit, that's just what we need. Devon, take over for me. I need to go upstairs with Karen and check the water," Jake called to his brother.

Keira rose from her stool and walked out to the hallway and the doorway leading to the internal staircase. Jake was already waiting for her. He let her go up first, and she could feel his eyes pinned to her ass. She couldn't help feeling more feminine and swaying her hips more than normal. She tried to stop, but her body just seemed to take over. She stepped back and waved a hand at the bathroom but didn't enter. Jake walked in and tried the faucets in the shower and the sink.

"I don't know what's going on, honey. There's probably a blockage in the pipes. I'm going to have to call a plumber in, but it's too late today. You know what tradesmen are like. I'll have to get onto it tomorrow. Why don't you pack your stuff up? You can stay at our house until we have the water problem sorted," Jake suggested.

"Uh, I don't…" Keira began.

"Come on, honey. I can't leave you here without any water. Come on down to the bar when you've finished packing your stuff and I'll get you that drink. Devon and I will finish our shift early tonight. We have a couple of staff coming in to close up the rest of the week. Besides, I don't like you staying here by yourself. It's not safe for a woman to be alone, especially at a club.

"I'll have the plumbers in tomorrow, and if you still want to come back here when the plumbing is fixed, then you can. But just know that if you do come back to the club, my brothers and I will take turns staying here as well. We want to know that you're safe," Jake said, coming out of the bathroom. "Tell me what you want to drink and I'll have it ready for you."

"A glass of Shiraz would be nice, thanks," Keira replied then headed to her room.

She didn't really want to impose on the Domain brothers, but she didn't have much of a choice, and she would feel a lot safer having three big, brawny men there to protect her. She couldn't survive without her morning and nightly showers. She loved to feel clean after spending a day in an office staring at a computer screen. Air-conditioning always played havoc with her skin, leaving her feeling grimy at the end of the day. Keira finished packing and took her stuff down to her car. She had to make two trips, but she was determined to do it herself. She was just heading to the front doors to the club when Devon came out the entrance. He had a scowl on his face which told her he was upset about something.

"What the hell are you doing, sweetheart?"

"I was putting my stuff in my car. What did it look like I was doing?" Keira replied belligerently.

"Don't you go getting sassy with me, little girl. Why didn't you wait and let us do that?" Devon asked.

Keira took in Devon's narrowed eyes and his aggressive stance. He stood there in front of her with his feet shoulder width apart, his hands on his hips, and his pelvis thrust forward. She had no idea what had crawled up his ass, but she wasn't letting him take his mood out on her.

"Why would I, Devon? I am a big girl and can take care of myself," Keira replied. She moved around him and could see he was having trouble controlling his anger. She could see the muscles in his arms striating with tension, and his jaw was ticking as he ground his teeth together. She turned back and entered the club. She kept on walking and sat down on the barstool she had earlier.

Keira watched Jake working the bar, and then moved toward her. He handed her a glass of Shiraz, and she took an appreciative sip. "Thanks, Jake."

"No problem, honey. Why didn't you let Devon and I help you with your stuff? And why have you put it in your car? I thought we could all drive back in my truck."

"I loaded my car with my stuff because I am quite capable of doing it. I'm not an invalid or a helpless airhead you know," Keira replied exasperatedly.

"I know you're not, honey, but we like to help. Next time you need stuff carried, call us," Jake stated quietly.

"Oh, for crying out loud, you're just as bad as your brother," Keira said and rolled her eyes.

She watched as Jake moved in closer to her. He leaned over the bar until she could feel his breath whispering against her lips.

"Actually, honey, I'm a lot worse than Devon is. And you'd better learn to do as you're told or Greg is gonna pitch a fit."

"What the hell is that supposed to mean?" Keira asked through clenched teeth.

Jake didn't answer, just shrugged his shoulders and took off to fill an order at the other end of the bar. What was it about these dominant, sexy men that turned her on so much?

Keira watched Devon and Jake work along the bar, chatting amicably with the customers. They seemed so open and friendly with the other people. She wondered why they hadn't been snapped up and married with kids. They had to be in their early to mid thirties in age. She knew if the women of Seattle had seen them they would have been well and truly off the market by now. They were sex gods with all their bulging muscles and excessive testosterone. Keira felt her pussy soften and her clit throb as she stared at them. Since she hadn't had a chance to shower and she'd left off her underwear, she could feel her jeans becoming damp. Her breasts felt heavy and swollen, her nipples hardened, and she looked down and saw them poking at the front of her T-shirt. She knew she should have taken time to dress properly.

"Penny for your thoughts, baby," a familiar voice rumbled into her ear.

Keira shivered as Greg's warm, moist breath caressed her ear. She turned her head and literally bumped lips with him. She felt her cheeks heat, and she turned her head away. She picked up her glass of red wine and took another sip.

"Are you ready to go?" Greg asked.

"How did you know I was coming back with you?" Keira asked and cringed mentally at the breathless quality of her own voice.

"Jake called me. By the time you finish your drink the others will be here to take over and we can go home," Greg said, and sat beside her.

Keira finally looked at Greg and could see the desire he felt for her in his eyes. She shifted on her stool and took another sip of her wine, hoping her contrived indifference would send his attention elsewhere. It didn't work though. He just sat staring at her.

"You're staring," Keira said as she turned back to look at Greg.

"You're very beautiful."

Keira choked on the sip of wine she'd just taken. She hadn't expected him to say that, and she wasn't flattered because she knew what he said was a lie. She wasn't beautiful at all. She was just as plain as they come.

"No I'm not, but thanks for saying so."

"How can you not see how gorgeous you are? You're not only beautiful on the outside but you are inside as well."

"How the hell did you come to that conclusion? You don't even know me."

"I know more about you than you think. Come on, let's go. Give me your keys and I'll drive your car," Greg requested, and he held his hand out for her keys.

Keira placed her now-empty wineglass on the bar, fished out a note, placed it under her glass, and turned toward Greg. She heard a growl behind her and turned to see Jake glaring at her. *Now what have I done?* She raised her eyebrow, silently questioning Jake. He pointed to the money she'd left, and when she just kept staring at him he picked up the money, jumped the bar, and tucked it back into the pocket of her jeans. She felt her knees weaken to see such a masculine display of strength and agility and hoped the heat she felt permeating her body didn't show.

Greg took the car keys from her hand and then took her empty hand in his. Jake slid his hand down her arm until he had her hand in his, and she felt another set of hands on her hips. She turned her head to see Devon behind her. She hadn't even seen him come back into the bar, but to have his hands on her sent her libido skyrocketing. She imagined what it would feel like to have all three men touching her at the same time. Her pussy clenched and dripped more of her cream. *What is wrong with me? Why the hell am I lusting after three men?*

"Let's take this beautiful woman home so she can get settled in," Jake said.

Keira had no other option than to follow as the three Domain men herded her toward the door.

When they were outside and heading to the vehicles, Greg stopped and sniffed the air. Keira heard him growl, a deep, rumbling sound that came up from the depths of his chest and out through his clenched teeth. He stepped in front of her, and Jake and Devon were both at her sides. She heard the doors to the club open behind her, and there were more bodies at her back. The sound of screeching tires coming across the parking lot made her cringe as she waited for the inevitable bang of a car accident, but the sound never came. She heard the car backfire, and then she was on the ground, her body covered by a mountain of muscle. She heard yelling and more blasts from the car, and then there was total silence. *Why can't I hear?* Her face was flush on the hard black surface, and she could feel gravel digging into her cheek. Her hip was aching from being ground into the hard asphalt beneath her, and she knew she was probably going to have a bruise and scrapes.

The weight on her eased off, and then she was in Devon's arms. Her ears were ringing, and she could see Devon's lips moving, but she couldn't hear him. *What the hell?* She frowned at him and placed her hands to her ears. She didn't want to speak in case she yelled everything. She saw the relief in his eyes as he looked at her, and then he hugged her tight against him. He picked her up and carried her back into the club and down the hallway which led to the office. His hands reached for her shirt, and he waited for her approval. She realized he wanted to make sure she wasn't hurt anywhere and gave him a nod.

He had her stripped naked in seconds, and he ran his hands all over her body. She couldn't get over the fact she was standing before Devon completely naked. Her ears were ringing which she knew was a good sign. Her hearing was coming back.

"Can you hear me now, sweetheart?" Devon asked.

"Yes. What the hell was that all about? Let me go. I'm fine," Keira stated and pulled her clothes back on. She was in such a hurry to cover herself she got caught up in her twisted T-shirt and couldn't get out.

"You are more than fine, sweetheart. Let me help you with that," Devon said, and then her T-shirt was on, covering her once more. "That was someone taking potshots at us."

"What? You mean someone was shooting at us?" The pitch of her voice escalated. She felt her knees wobble and reached up with a shaky hand to push her hair back from her face.

"Come here, sweetheart," Devon said and pulled her over to him as he sat down on the sofa. She ended up sitting on his lap. He wrapped his arms around her and hugged her tight against him, but not tight enough that he hurt her. She clung to him. Keira could feel her body shaking and was glad for the warmth and comfort the haven of Devon's big body offered. It had been so long since she'd been held. She savored the sensation of having his big body surrounding hers.

"Yes, someone was shooting at us," Devon finally answered.

Keira felt the blood drain from her face. Surely David hadn't found her already. God, she had to get out of here. The last thing she wanted to do was put the three men kind enough to offer her a job and somewhere to live in danger.

"It's okay, sweetheart. You have nothing to be afraid of. We'll protect you," Devon stated.

"Oh God. What about Jake and Greg? Did they get hurt? Shit. I have to go," Keira said, pushing against Devon's arms.

"Settle down, baby. We're fine," Greg said.

Keira turned her head toward the door and saw Greg and Jake walking into the room. They looked really mad, and she hoped that anger wasn't directed at her.

"Are you hurt, honey?" Jake asked and rubbed her on the arm.

"No, I'm fine. Who was shooting at you? What are you guys into?" Keira asked as she finally managed to get off Devon's lap and backed away from the three men staring at her. She didn't stop until her back connected with the wall.

"Did you check her over, Devon?" Greg asked.

"Yes. She has a bruise on her left hip which was probably from me pushing her into the ground and a small graze on her cheek. Other than that she is fine."

"Stop talking about me as if I'm not here," Keira said in frustration. She whimpered as Greg turned to her and pinned her in place with his eyes. She felt like a mouse about to become prey to a cat.

Greg didn't stop until he had her caged in. He placed his arms on either side of her head and pressed his body along the length of hers. She could feel his hard cock pressing into her stomach. "They weren't after us, baby. They were after you. But you already knew that, didn't you, Keira?"

Keira felt her legs buckle beneath her. Greg caught her before she could hit the floor. She gasped as Greg picked her up into his arms and slanted his mouth over hers. The sensation of his body against hers and the heat he was emanating was unbelievable. She whimpered when he thrust his tongue into her mouth and slid it along hers. He had her from simmering to boiling in moments. She responded tentatively at first then moaned as his hand cupped her breast and he flicked his thumb across her cotton-covered nipple. Keira screamed with pleasure as her cunt clenched and spasmed. She rode out the pleasure as she clutched at Greg's massive, bulging biceps.

Keira hid her face against Greg's chest, too embarrassed to look him in the eyes. She couldn't believe she had just climaxed from a kiss and having her nipple rubbed. She squealed in surprise when Greg scooped her up in his arms and headed for the door.

"Let's get our woman home," Greg said.

Keira peeked over his shoulder and saw Jake and Devon eyeing her with fire in their eyes. What had she gotten herself into?

Chapter Six

"What do you mean *your* woman?"

"We are all attracted to you, Keira. We knew eventually that we would want to share a woman between us. You are that woman, baby," Greg replied.

"What? What the hell do you mean you want to share me?"

"Just that, baby. We want you in our lives and in our bed. We won't force you, Keira, but just think about how good it would be. I know you want us, too. I can smell your sweet pussy creaming whenever we are close to you."

"Oh God," Keira muttered and squirmed in her seat. Could she really let them touch her? She had never responded to any male before. She was very attracted to the Domain brothers, but didn't know if she could do what they wanted. She sighed as her mind ran around in circles of turmoil and confusion.

Keira sat in the passenger seat of her car as Greg drove. She would have liked to see where she was going, but it was dark now and they had left the lights of Aztec behind. She wanted to ask how they knew who she was, but didn't have the guts. The last thing she wanted was to start an argument in the car when she wasn't in control of the steering wheel. She knew she had control issues. She'd been told by some of her friends as well as her own brother that she was way too anal over the simplest of things.

Ever since her parents had died, she had kept a tight rein on herself and her emotions. She was scared to let go and live. She was scared of losing people she cared about and had tried to keep them at arm's length. But only with her friends. She couldn't do that to her brother. He was the one keeping his distance. She had tried for years to get his love but nothing she did ever seemed to work. She knew it was her way of dealing with the grief of losing her parents at a young age. The only time she ever felt in complete control was when she was doing the books. She loved working with numbers. She was passionate about her job and didn't care the few real friends she had thought she was a nerd. So she had worked hard and spent most of her time doing books. She had pushed her friends away and lived to work, rather than working to live, not that she really needed to financially, but she hated being idle and felt more in control when she was busy.

Keira sat up straighter in her seat when Greg slowed the car down and turned into a driveway. A massive iron gate blocked the drive. She watched as Greg wound down the window and pushed an intercom button on a small speaker box. She heard a male's voice asking who wanted entry, and when Greg replied, the gates began to open.

"The gates are automatic. We all have an infrared device in our cars which operates the gates. I'll see that you get one fitted in your car," Greg stated.

She remained quiet as Greg drove up the gravel track and held her breath when the house finally came into view. It was the most beautiful sight she'd ever seen. The house was massive in proportion. There were large white stone columns on either side of the front door, and the roof over the entry sheltered it from the weather.

She looked at her surroundings as Greg drove the car past the front of the house and around to the other side. He pulled her rusted-up heap into a large carport and turned the ignition off. She turned when she felt his eyes on her.

"You will be safe here, Keira. Come on and I'll get you settled in. Then I can introduce you to everyone," Greg stated and got out of the car.

Keira took another deep breath and let it out. She felt as if her life were about to change forever, but she pushed that thought aside and castigated herself for letting her imagination run wild. She got out of the car, and Greg took her hand in his. She turned at the sound of another vehicle and watched as Jake and Devon drove up and parked behind her bomb. Great, now she couldn't even get her car out if she wanted to. She was going to have to ask them to move their truck first. She felt trapped, and she couldn't see a way out. Her breathing escalated, and she felt sweat bead on her forehead. Her heart was pounding in her chest a mile a minute, and she felt her hand shaking in Greg's.

"Keira, look at me," Greg said gently.

Keira looked up into Greg's eyes and felt herself drowning. His eyes were flashing from brown to gold and back again. *What the hell?* She knew she wasn't imagining this time. *What are these people?* She pulled her hand from Greg's and backed away. She came to an abrupt stop when she bumped into a large, warm chest. She turned her head and tilted her chin to look up into Jake's green eyes. *Shit. His eyes are flashing, too.* She stepped to the side, but Devon was there. His irises were flashing from hazel to gold as well. *I am so out of here.*

Keira ducked around Devon and took off. She hadn't taken three steps before she was stopped. Greg stood in front of her, his hands lightly on her hips keeping her still.

"We would never hurt you, Keira. Please, don't be afraid of us," Greg said.

"What the hell are you people?" Keira wasn't surprised to hear the fear in her own voice. She shivered when she felt a warm body at her back, and she looked into Devon's eyes when he came to stand at her side.

"We are werewolves, Keira, and you are our mate," Devon replied.

Keira felt her breath hitch at Devon's statement. She'd always wanted to believe there were other kinds of humans on the planet, but had never thought she'd confirm her hypothesis. She looked at Devon and just knew he was telling the truth. How else had their eyes been changing if they weren't what he'd said? Then the last of his words sank in. She was their mate! *Fuck that.* She couldn't be the mate to three men.

"No. I'm not your mate," Keira said. "I can't be a mate to three men…werewolves."

"I assure you, you are our mate, Keira," Greg reiterated. "Come on inside. We'll discuss this when you're settled."

Keira wanted to turn tail and run. But she also wanted to explore her connection with the three brothers. God, she didn't even know her own mind anymore. She followed Greg as he gently tugged her hand and led her to a door off the carport. Her jeans were soaking wet, and she craved the touch of their hands, mouths, and cocks. *What is wrong with me? I'm turning into a slut.*

She looked around as Greg led her inside. The place could have graced any home magazine and won house of the year. It was so much more tasteful than her home back in Seattle. She stumbled a little then slammed up against Greg's back. She felt one of his brothers steady her with a hand at her waist. Greg pulled her out from behind him to his side. They were standing in a large hallway, and three strange, handsome men stared at her and the Domain brothers. They were all so tall, muscular, and sexy, but as far as she was concerned they didn't hold a candle to Greg, Jake, and Devon.

"Alphas, I'd like you to meet our mate, Keira O'Lachlan. Keira, these three men are the Alphas, leaders of the pack, Jonah, Mikhail, and Brock Friess. You can meet their mate a little later," Greg stated.

"I am pleased to meet you, Keira. I hope you'll be happy here," Jonah said.

Keira didn't know what to do, but she knew she was probably supposed to be submissive in the Alphas' presence. She'd read enough erotic romance novels to be aware of some of the protocol. She lowered her eyes and nodded her head at the three dominant men.

"I'm pleased to meet you all," she said.

"Go and get your mate settled in. Dinner should be ready by the time you're done. Since Keira obviously knows what we are, I'll expect you three on our run tonight. She can stay with Michelle," Jonah stated.

"At your command, Alpha," Greg replied. "Come, Keira."

"I'm not a dog, you know. You can't just command me like I am," Keira said as she was pulled along by Greg.

"I know you're not, baby. I just want you settled in," Greg replied.

Keira followed Greg up the wide flight of stairs to the third level. He turned right and led her down the long carpeted hall. He stopped outside of the door at the end and opened it, ushering her through. Keira gasped as she took in the large living area with the bulky leather furniture. There was a doorway off to the side which she presumed led to the bedrooms.

Greg led her to that door and turned door handles left and right as he went along the hall. "This is Devon's room. This is Jake's, and this one is mine. The bathroom is at the end of the hall and the toilet is enclosed off the bathroom. I have another bathroom off my room."

"So I'll be sleeping on the sofa then?" Keira asked hopefully.

Greg spun around, placed his hands at her waist, and picked her up until her eyes were level with his.

"No, baby girl, you'll be sleeping in my bed," Greg said in a steely voice.

"No. I won't," Keira replied.

"Yes, you will," Greg reiterated. He kissed her lightly on the lips and lowered her until her feet were back on the floor. "Look around as much as you want. We're going to unload your stuff. We'll be back before you know it."

"Don't hurry on my account," Keira muttered under her breath and stomped back to the living room. She decided she was going to be childish. Since Greg had told her to explore she was going to do the exact opposite.

"I heard that, baby." Greg's voice followed her.

Keira didn't care. She just shrugged her shoulders and kept right on going. She threw herself onto the navy-blue sofa and crossed her arms over her chest. She didn't care if she looked like a spoiled brat. Her world had been turned upside down. She thought she was entitled to feel a little piqued. She was glad when they left the rooms.

Keira was still sitting on the sofa when she heard a knock on the door. She looked up to see a beautiful, slender, green-eyed woman walking toward her with a welcoming smile.

"Hi, you must be Keira. I'm Michelle Barclay, soon to be Friess. I imagine you're feeling a little overwhelmed right now," Michelle said as she sat down in an armchair opposite Keira.

"That would be the understatement of the year," Keira muttered. Then she realized Michelle had heard her when the woman burst out laughing. "Sorry, I didn't mean to be disrespectful."

"Hey, don't worry about it. We women have to stick together. The men in this pack are so arrogant and dominant they'd take you over if you let them," Michelle said.

"Too late, they already have. So are you mated to more than one man?" Keira asked then covered her mouth at her rude, blunt question. "Sorry again. I don't know what's gotten into me. I'm not usually so blunt."

"Don't worry about it. You can ask me anything. And the answer is yes. I'm mated to Jonah, Mikhail, and Brock."

"Wow. So you're like a queen or something?" Keira asked.

"That's what they call me. But to me I'm still just the local librarian," Michelle stated. "I've only been here for about six months. So everything is still so new to me. I still have a lot to learn about pack protocol. But if you have any questions, go right ahead and ask. I'll answer them if I can."

"To be honest, I don't know what I'm doing here. I only started working at the Aztec Club yesterday. And today, here I am. They only just told me that they're werewolves and I'm their mate. How the hell am I supposed to deal with that?" Keira asked and rose to her feet.

She began pacing with agitation. She could feel hysteria rising up within her, but took a few deep, calming breaths and pushed it back down.

"Actually, I'd have to say you're dealing with everything a lot better than I did," Michelle said.

"Really?"

"Yeah. I sort of got a little hysterical. If it hadn't been for the fact I'd just been given pain medication, I would have run screaming."

"They hurt you?" Keira asked incredulously.

"No. My mates would never hurt me. I had a little accident on the stairs and broke my wrist," Michelle explained.

"Shit, I bet that hurt."

"Like you wouldn't believe. I can see all those questions rattling around in your head. Ask me anything you like," Michelle said.

"How the hell do you mate with three men?" Keira blurted out, but didn't apologize this time. She needed to know for her own sanity.

"The men have to bite you for their wolves to stake their claim, and you have sex," Michelle answered.

"Did they claim you all at the same time?" Keira asked nervously.

"No. They did it separately," Michelle answered. "But let me tell you, when we all have sex together, it's out of this world."

"You mean you… In the…and all together?"

"Yeah," Michelle answered. And by the sappy look on her face and her glazed eyes, the woman really loved ménages.

"How does the pack hierarchy work?" Keira queried.

"My mates are all Alphas of the pack, but Jonah is lead Alpha. If he decides to put his foot down, then his final word is Pack Law. He, Mikhail, and Brock have the ability to use their voices to control their minions. They are so hot when they do that," Michelle grinned.

"If I decide to let them claim me, does that mean I will be a werewolf, too?" Keira asked.

"No. You will have slightly enhanced abilities. You will heal much faster and your sight and hearing will be more acute. From the information I have gathered, the only way to change a human to a werewolf is brutal and painful. It isn't done though because the risks are too great, and the human could die. Oh, and your mates won't want to be away from you for longer than a day, and they want sex regularly."

"How regularly?" Keira asked.

"As much as they can get from you," Michelle replied with a grin. "Trust me. You'll love it. Now, I need to get downstairs. Dinner's almost ready. Oh, here come your mates. I'll leave you to it," Michelle said and left with a wave.

Sure enough, moments later, Greg, Devon, and Jake entered the room, their arms full of her stuff. They walked through the living room and disappeared down the hall, presumably to Greg's room. They were back moments later.

"Let's go get some dinner," Jake said and helped her from the sofa.

Keira followed along, not knowing what else to do. She was in a situation she had no control over and felt as if she were in a boat adrift at sea. Maybe she should just go along for the ride and see what happened.

Chapter Seven

Keira was seated at a long table in a dining room on the other side of the kitchen counter. She had followed the men down to the ground floor, and they had led her to a doorway to the right of the entrance hall. The room was huge, but she supposed it had to be, on account of all the people seated around the table. She was sitting between Jake and Greg. Greg was sitting to the right of Mikhail, and Jake was sitting to her right. There weren't many women at the table. She could see a sophisticated blonde talking to a large man on her left who must be her mate, judging by the way they were all over each other. She could see another woman sitting near the other end of the table, and the only others were Michelle and the two women in the kitchen. The house was full of testosterone-laden males. She leaned over and whispered in Jake's ear.

"Why are there only a few women here?"

"We're not really sure, honey. There have been fewer and fewer females being born to the pack over the last couple of generations. Most of our elders are off enjoying their retirement away from pack responsibility now that Jonah and his brothers have taken over rule," Jake answered.

"So none of these men have mates?"

"No. Most of them are still single."

Jonah's voice drew her attention away from Jake, and she looked over to see him standing at the head of the table. Michelle was seated beside him, but she didn't make an effort to stand, so Keira stayed seated as well.

"Everyone, I would like to introduce you to Keira O'Lachlan. She is the mate of Greg, Jake, and Devon. Keira, everyone will introduce themselves to you at their leisure. It will be easier for you to remember names if you are told a few at a time. Welcome to Friess Pack," Jonah said and then sat down.

Keira nodded her head in respect, but she was silently fuming. She wasn't a part of their pack. What the hell had the Domain men told their Alphas? She hadn't told any of the men claiming to be her mates she was going to accept them. Did they think they could ride roughshod over her and take what they wanted without asking? Well, she had news for them, and it was all bad.

Keira was glad when dinner was finally over and the men began to leave the room. Greg, Jake, and Devon each kissed her on the cheek before they left. Michelle stood and came over to her.

"The men are going for a run in their wolf form. Would you like to come and watch them go through the change?"

"I don't know if I'm ready for that yet," Keira replied honestly.

"I know how you feel. I'm still not used to seeing my mates in their animal form. Why don't we go through to the living room and share a bottle of wine?" Michelle suggested.

"Sure. Thanks, I'd really like that," Keira replied, following Michelle from the room.

"I don't know if I can do this, Michelle," Keira blurted out once they were seated on the sofa, each holding a glass of wine.

"What would that be? Having sex with three hot men or living here as a pack member?" Michelle asked.

"All of it."

"Your mates are good men, Keira. Why fight the attraction you feel toward them? And don't bother denying it. I can see it on your face and in your eyes that you want them. Why not just take one day at a time and see what happens?"

"That's just it, Michelle. I never just go with the flow. Until recently I planned my day out to every waking moment. I don't know how to be laid-back and just let things happen."

"Oh, believe me, I know what you're talking about. If you had told me seven months ago I was going to be mated to three men, I would have told you that you were off your rocker. You see, I had hidden my true self beneath the façade of an uptight, old-maid librarian. I was too scared to be myself. Is it so wrong to have three men love you? No, I don't think so. In fact it is the best thing that could have ever happened to me.

"I think you are a lot like me. You've regimented yourself for some reason, and buried the real you underneath all that control. Would it be so bad to give that control over to the three men who could love you and change your world for the better? I'm not trying to say you have to do what I did and accept those three men as your mates. But think about how you would feel if they were no longer a part of your life."

Keira sipped at her wine as she thought over what Michelle had said. Was she really that uptight that she could no longer be spontaneous? If it hadn't been for hearing her brother on the phone she would still be living in her deceased parents' house, making her lists, and working on other people's books. She had buried her real self underneath all that control. She hadn't even realized it until now. She knew she was anal about a lot of things, but she had become even more so since the death of her parents. She felt as if her whole world had shattered. To know her brother had killed her parents was so far beyond her comprehension. Why would he do that to the people who had taken him and loved him as if he were their own?

Keira felt a tear leak from the corner of her eye and slip down her face. Another and another followed along, until she was sobbing quietly. She felt Michelle take her wineglass, and then she hugged her. The sound of wolves howling in the night made her jump, but she was too caught up in her own emotions to think anything of it. She cried for her lost parents, for her deceitful, murdering brother, and she cried for herself. She'd tried so hard to be a good sister and a good person. She had wanted her brother to love her, but she knew that just wasn't possible.

Keira felt Michelle unwind her arms from around her, and then she was being lifted up against a hard, warm, muscular chest. She burrowed her head into Greg's shoulder, his familiar scent enveloping her in comfort. She knew they were moving. She felt his muscles rippling beneath her cheek, but she just wanted to hide. Moments later she was laid down on a soft mattress and surrounded on all sides by large, hard, warm bodies. Her crying slowed, her tears finally drying up, but she still kept her face hidden.

* * * *

Greg and his brothers had been enjoying the freedom of running through the trees in their wolf form. His Alpha Jonah had run up to his side and spoken to him telepathically.

"Your mate is upset and needs you," Jonah had said in Greg's mind.

Greg had changed direction immediately and headed back to the house. He'd felt a knot of fear forming in his chest and wanted to be with Keira, holding her in his arms so he knew she was safe and sound.

"Jake, Devon, Keira needs us, get back to the house," Greg had commanded his brothers through their private link.

Greg had run to where he'd left his clothes, changed back from his wolf, and gotten dressed. He had been heading toward the back door of the house when he'd scented his brothers. He didn't wait for them though. He'd needed to see and hold Keira then. The sight of his mate crying quietly in the arms of his queen had nearly broken his heart. He was so relieved that she was where he could hold her and know she was safe. Even the pipes in the club's upstairs bathroom had helped bring her home to him and his brothers. He'd moved in and picked Keira up into his arms and headed for their suite of rooms. The fact that his mate didn't make any noise when she was crying had told him she was still keeping part of herself hidden. He sighed with relief when her crying had slowed, her breath hitching for the last time, but still she'd kept her face hidden as he had lain down with her on his bed. His brothers had entered the room, and they had gotten onto the bed, surrounding their mate.

"Look at me, Keira," Greg said quietly. He waited until Keira lifted her head, and the sight of her red, swollen eyes and her pain clutched at his heart. "Why were you crying?"

He watched as Keira tried to push away from him, but he wouldn't let her. He helped her to sit up on his lap and wrapped his arms around her waist loosely.

"I think my brother is trying to kill me. I think he killed my parents, too. No, I know he did. I heard him talking on the phone and he said he'd get rid of me just like he did my parents," Keira said and began to cry again.

"Ah, baby girl. I'd take your pain away if I could," Greg said and pulled her into his body. He just held her as she cried out her grief and pain. When she was done for the moment he picked her up and carried her to the bathroom. "You're going to have a bath and relax while we take care of you. All right?"

Greg waited for Keira to respond and sighed with relief when she nodded. He sat down on the rim of the huge bathtub and turned the water on. He slowly began to remove her clothes and was surprised when she didn't protest. The sight of her nude body had his cock going hard and his wolf pushing at him to claim her, but he knew she wasn't ready for that. He stood up and gently lowered her into the filling tub, then began to strip off his own clothes. He climbed into the bath with her and pulled her on his lap. He looked up when Jake and Devon walked into the bathroom, removed their clothes, and hopped into the tub with him and Keira. He held her while his brothers washed her from head to foot. He knew she was enjoying being pampered for a change because he heard her sigh and she was relaxed against him. Once his brothers were finished washing her, Greg picked her up and stepped out of the tub. He held her until she had her feet on the floor and gently patted her dry. He handed her over to Jake since his brother was already dry and began to dry off as Jake carried Keira back to his bedroom.

Greg smiled when he saw Keira snuggled in his bed with Jake. He let his eyes travel down the length of her delicious nude body and felt his cock jerk in reaction. She was so damn sexy. He wanted to crawl between her thighs and lap the cream her could smell leaking from her pussy. He knew he and his brothers wouldn't be able to keep their wolves at bay much longer. They needed to claim their mate. He wanted to do it now and knew he couldn't stop himself from trying. He only hoped Keira would be receptive to the idea.

Greg climbed on the bottom of his king-size bed and smoothed his hands up over Keira's calves. When she didn't pull away, he slid them up further to her knees. He gently parted her thighs and moved his body up between her now-spread legs. The scent of her juices had a growl rumbling up from his chest. He bent his head and took the first taste of his mate's delectable cunt.

Greg slid his tongue through her drenched folds from clit to ass and back again. With the first taste, he knew he would never get enough. He slid his shoulders between her legs and lay on his belly. He wrapped his arms around her thighs, spreading her legs wide, and devoured her. He thrust his tongue in and out of her, collecting and swallowing her scrumptious cream. He massaged over her clit with the tip of his tongue as he rimmed her cunt with his finger. He slid the tip of his digit into her body and felt her muscles contract around his flesh. He lapped, laved, and sucked on Keira's clit, pushing his finger into her body a little more with every forward thrust. He hesitated when his finger was in nearly all the way.

He felt her hymen stretch, and possessiveness consumed him. The knowledge that Keira hadn't been intimate with anyone else filled him with joy. He withdrew his finger slightly, sucked her clit into his mouth, and stretched the membrane. The sound of Keira sobbing out with pleasure as she climaxed and gripped his finger made his balls draw up tight to his body. The sensation of her cream covering his flesh and her internal walls gripping and releasing pushed him over the edge. He sat up between her thighs and gently gripped her hips.

The sight of her kissing Jake and Devon suckling on one of her nipples had his wolf pushing for control. He had to claim his mate. Greg aimed his cock for Keira's cunt and began to push in. She pulled her mouth from Jake's and arched her neck and bucked her hips up at his. He groaned as he slid another few inches into her tight, wet pussy. He held still and breathed rapidly, trying to keep his wolf at bay and to give Keira time to adjust to his intrusion, but she wouldn't let him.

"Greg, please," Keira sobbed.

"Please what, baby?"

"Fuck me!" Keira yelled.

Greg glided his cock back a couple of inches, then thrust into Keira's pussy until he felt his balls connect with her ass. He nudged his brothers aside and covered her body with his. He licked down her neck until he reached the place where it met her shoulder. He let his canines elongate, and he bit down through her skin and flesh. He heard Keira scream, and she writhed beneath him as she climaxed. He withdrew his teeth as they retreated back into his gums and licked the mark he'd made on his mate. He shifted to his knees between her splayed thighs and began to fuck his woman.

Greg groaned as he pumped his hips, his cock sliding in and out of Keira's tight, wet cunt. He looked into her passion-glazed eyes as he picked up the pace of his rocking hips. He leaned down and took her mouth under his own and thrust his tongue into her depths. Her wet heat surrounding his hard cock was so good. He knew he wouldn't last much longer. He could already feel the tingle at the base of his spine. He moved one of his hands between their joined bodies, running it downward until he reached to top of her slit and began to rub lightly on her clit. She mewled and arched her hips up into his, meeting his every forward thrust. He suckled on her tongue and gently pinched her little nub between his thumb and finger. She cried out as her internal pussy walls clamped down around his hard cock. Her muscles clenching and releasing was enough to send him over with her. He felt his balls draw up, and then he was filling her with his seed. His wolf howled with possessive pleasure, and Greg collapsed down on top of Keira, leaning on his elbows so he wouldn't crush her. He reached up, took her face between his hands, and kissed her. He had claimed his mate.

Chapter Eight

Keira couldn't believe she'd just had sex for the first time, with one man while his brothers helped to pleasure her. She lay on the bed totally naked, her muscles so weak from the pleasure of fucking Greg that she knew she wouldn't be able to move. She grinned and wondered why she didn't want to try sex before. She had so been missing out. The persistent voice in her head butted into her thoughts. *You didn't have sex because you weren't in love before, silly. Oh no. I am so not going there. I don't even know these men. Then what are you doing, girl?*

"Are you okay, baby?" Greg asked as he gently withdrew his cock from her body.

"Yeah," Keira answered and recoiled at the sound of her breathy voice. Greg moved off the bed and headed for the bathroom. She looked up at Jake when he cupped her cheek with his large palm.

"Are you ready for more, honey?" Jake asked.

Keira felt her eyes widen at Jake's question. She wasn't sure if she could take any more. All she wanted to do was curl up and go to sleep.

"I don't know," Keira replied honestly.

"Will you let me kiss you? If you don't want any more loving tonight, then that's okay. But I need to feel your sweet lips under mine," Jake stated.

"Okay," Keira replied. She couldn't understand it, since she'd just had three amazing orgasms, but her pussy clenched with need at the words Jake painted in her mind. She stared into his green eyes as he lowered his mouth to hers.

Keira moaned as his lips slid over hers and his tongue licked over her bottom lip. The act was so sensual she arched her chest up, wanting, needing to connect with Jake flesh to flesh. His tongue slipped in between her lips, sliding along hers, and she nipped lightly with her teeth. The sound of his growl rumbling out into her mouth made her pussy clench with desire.

Jake weaned his mouth from hers and eased her over onto her side, her back now along the length of his front. She looked up at Devon and saw the heat in his eyes as he stared at her, but Jake drew her attention back to him when he lifted her leg up and back, placing her thigh over his hip. He ran his fingers through her sopping pussy, collecting her juices, and began to massage her sensitive clit with the tip of his fingers. She pushed her ass back at him, begging him to fill her with his cock. Her flaring embers were now a raging inferno, and she needed him buried in her cunt. He slid his fingers back down through her wet folds, and she flinched when she felt one of his fingers massaging her ass.

"Sh, honey. I won't hurt you, I promise. Just relax and let yourself feel. If you don't like anything I do, just say so and I'll stop," Jake whispered against her ear.

When she felt the mattress dip, Keira opened her eyes and stared into Devon's. He was now lying down facing her. He reached down and began to massage her clit with light circles. The sensation of having two different hands from two different brothers on her body was an aphrodisiac in itself. Her raging desire burned even higher.

She felt Jake collecting more of her cream, and then his finger was pushing into her ass. There was a slight pinch and burn, but the pain only seemed to enhance her pleasure. He began to withdraw his finger from her anus, but she didn't want him to. She clenched her ass around him as she sobbed out her frustration.

"Easy, honey. I'll give you what you need. Keep those muscles relaxed for me, Keira," Jake whispered.

Keira heard a popping sound, and then his fingers were back on the sensitive skin of her little pucker. He must have grabbed some lube because the moisture on his fingers was cold. She whimpered as he pushed two digits into her ass and moaned as her reflexive muscles clamped down on his flesh.

"Breathe deeply and evenly, sweetheart. Jake needs to stretch that pretty little asshole so he doesn't hurt you," Devon said.

Keira knew then that Jake and Devon planned to fuck her at the same time. She didn't know if she could handle that. She was worried they would rip her apart. She'd seen the size of their cocks and wasn't sure she could handle one of those in her ass. She looked up to Devon and knew he could see her uncertainty. He leaned over her and took her lips under his. There was no preliminary with Devon. He opened his mouth and took what he wanted. He swept his tongue into her cavern, slid it along hers and into every part of her maw. He consumed her with his mouth, and she gave herself over to him.

Jake was still stretching her ass, and Devon was devouring her mouth as well as rubbing her clit. Keira could feel her internal muscles beginning to coil. Her womb was heavy with her liquid desire, and she was only moments away from climaxing again. She mewed as they withdrew their fingers and mouth from her body. She heard the popping sound again and knew Jake was getting ready to fuck her ass.

"Breathe out for me, honey," Jake said.

Keira felt the head of his cock against the pucker of her ass. She concentrated on trying to keep her muscles lax, but it was hard. She whimpered as he began to push the crown of his hard rod into her anus. The burning, stretching pain of her tight muscles was almost more than she could bear. She opened her eyes, frantically searching out Devon. He must have seen the desperation in her eyes because he leaned over and took one of her breasts into his mouth. The sensation of having one of her nipples sucked while Jake gently forged his big cock into her ass nearly had her toppling over the edge. Her cunt clenched, and liquid cream slipped from her body to coat her thigh. Jake's litany in her ear made her clamp down on him even more.

"Honey, you have the tightest, sweetest ass. I can feel you clenching all around me. Use your muscles to push me out, Keira."

Keira did as Jake said, and she moaned as his big cock slid all the way into her ass. He surprised her by rolling over onto his back, taking her with him so that she was lying on top of him. He spread her legs with his own as he licked and nibbled his way down her neck.

"Keira, I'm going to slide into your tight, wet pussy. If it's too much, let me know, sweetheart," Devon stated.

Keira looked up to see Devon moving between her and Jake's splayed thighs. The sight of his huge cock bobbing as he moved made her pussy clench with anticipation and trepidation. He eased his body down on hers and kissed her mouth, then sat back up between her legs. The sight of him grasping his own huge rod, pumping along the length of his shaft with his own hand, was such a turn-on.

"You want some of this, don't ya, sweetness?" Devon said and eased the head of his cock up to the entrance of her cunt.

Keira couldn't answer. She was on fire and needed Jake and Devon to put out the flames. She moaned as Devon pushed the head of his cock into her body and couldn't help clenching around the two cocks now fighting for room.

"God, sweetness. You are so fucking tight and wet," Devon groaned.

Keira whimpered as Devon forged his way slowly and gently into her body. He stopped when she felt his balls flush on the cheeks of her ass.

"Are you ready, honey? Are you ready for your mates to claim you?" Jake growled into her ear.

"Yes. Yes. Please?"

"Please what, sweetness?" Devon asked as he wiggled his hips.

The sensation of Devon moving his cock around in her cunt was so good she needed more.

"Please, fuck me!" Keira screamed.

Devon slid his cock from her wet cunt and pushed back in. As he pushed in Jake clasped her hips and pulled his hard rod from her ass. The two men set up a slide and glide, advance and retreat which had her thrashing between them. She was so hot and turned on she could feel sweat forming on her brow. She felt the bed dip at her side and turned her head to see Greg pulling at his own hard cock beside her. He was lying on the bed on his side pleasuring himself. He reached over and tweaked a nipple between his thumb and fingcr. Thc sight of him sliding his own hand up and down his hard shaft made her mouth water for a taste. She reached over, wrapped her hand around his massive erection, and pulled him toward her.

Keira opened her mouth and twirled her tongue over the slit in his cock. His salty pre-cum coating her tongue made her crave more of his essence. She opened her mouth wide and sucked the head of his dick into her mouth.

"Fuck yeah, baby. That's it. Suck my dick," Greg moaned.

Keira was overwhelmed by all the pleasure being bestowed on her by the three men and knew she wasn't going to last long. She sucked Greg in as far as she could go without choking, hollowed her cheeks, and slid back up the length of his cock. She was being fucked in all her holes.

Jake and Devon were now pumping their hips into her body. Their cocks were gliding in and out of her ass and pussy. The sound of their flesh slapping against hers echoed through the room. Her pelvic-floor muscles were gathering closer and tighter, and she didn't know if she would be able to stand the pleasure. She writhed between the two men as she sucked on Greg's cock. She moaned when she felt Jake and Devon licking down her neck, and then she was flying. She screamed out, the sound muffled by Greg's cock, as they bit down into her flesh, her internal muscles contracting as she flew toward the stars. She heard them both howl, and then they filled her with their cum. Each spurt from their cocks just sent her higher and higher. Greg roared, and then she was swallowing frantically so she wouldn't choke on his semen. She swallowed every drop and groaned as he pulled his cock from her mouth. She shuddered and shook until the last spasm died, leaving her feeling like a big blob of jelly. The sound of their heavy breathing was the only noise in the room.

Since the Domain brothers had claimed her, she felt a deep connection to them. Keira was worried about the way the three men were burrowing their way into her heart, but didn't know if what she felt was love.

Chapter Nine

Keira was downstairs ready for breakfast the next morning before her men. She knew she probably had a sappy look on her face because she couldn't stop smiling, but she didn't care. She'd woken up surrounded by the heat emanating from the three men who had claimed her as their mate and hoped she would wake up that way every day for the rest of her life. She wondered why her hearing and eyesight seemed enhanced and then remembered Michelle telling her it would be. She knew she wasn't going to turn into a werewolf now that they had claimed her, and was thankful for that because she couldn't see herself turning furry and sniffing other wolves' butts. Since she didn't have to worry over that situation, she gave a mental shrug.

Breakfast was already on the table when she entered the room, so she took a seat and began to load her plate. The activities from last night left her stomach grumbling and begging to be filled.

"Keira, where are your mates?" Jonah asked her with a slight smile.

"In bed asleep," Keira replied.

Everyone around the table burst out laughing, and Keira felt her cheeks heat with embarrassment. They obviously knew what she and her mates had gotten up to last night.

"Don't worry about them, Keira," Michelle said. "They all have warped senses of humor."

Keira didn't reply. She gave a negligent shrug and lowered her eyes. She had nearly finished her eggs and toast when Greg came running into the room. He was stark naked, and his hair was standing on end. He looked so sexy. She couldn't prevent the gasp escaping her mouth. He pinned her to her seat with her eyes.

"Why are you down here, mate?" Greg growled.

Keira couldn't believe he had come into the dining room totally naked. He didn't seem to care that everyone could see his cock. She lowered her eyes and watched with fascination as his cock twitched and began to fill with blood. She felt her cheeks heat even more, but she couldn't take her eyes off him. She let her gaze wander the length of his body, and her pussy gushed out her liquid desire, dampening her panties. His body was so packed full of muscle. He was breathtaking. His muscles rippled as his body tensed, and within the blink of an eye he was at her side. He picked her up from her chair and slung her over his shoulder. He carried her from the room, catcalls and whistles following their departure.

"What the hell are you doing? Are you out of your mind? They all saw your cock. How could you embarrass me like that?" Keira rattled off quickly.

"I am taking you back to bed, baby. You shouldn't have left without letting one of us know where you were going," Greg stated and tapped her on the ass.

"Ow, that hurt."

"They've all seen my cock before, baby. I'm a werewolf, remember. I have to take my clothes off when I change forms, otherwise I'd be buying a new wardrobe of clothes every week," Greg said.

"Oh. Well, I don't like it that the other women get to ogle your body," Keira said.

"Okay, I'll try to keep my body out of sight of the other women, but sometimes it's just not possible, baby."

"Where are you taking me?"

"I would have thought that was obvious," Greg replied.

"Put me down, Greg. I can't," Keira said, struggling to get down.

Keira gave a sigh of relief as her lowered her from his shoulder. Her bare feet hit the mattress, and she was grateful when he steadied her by holding her waist.

"Are you sore, honey?" Jake's voice came from behind her.

Keira turned her head and stared as Jake and Devon slid their hands up and down their massive cocks. She could not believe she'd had Jake's dick in her ass.

"Of course I'm sore. I had those monsters in my body," Keira retorted and rolled her eyes.

Keira turned her head back to Greg when he took her chin in his hand.

"You are not to leave this room without telling one of us where you're going," Greg commanded quietly.

"Why? I'm safe here, aren't I?"

"Of course you are, baby. We just like to know where you are," he replied.

"So even if I have to go pee, you want to know about it?" Keira asked, placing her hands on her hips with indignation.

"Well, no. You don't have to go that far, Keira. Don't you go getting sassy with me, little girl. I only have your best interests and safety at heart," Greg said and began to unbutton her shirt. He had her blouse and bra off in moments.

"What are you doing?"

"I'm undressing you, baby," Greg answered with a smile.

"I know that, duh. But why? I've already told you I can't," Keira replied.

"I know you're sore, Keira, but I need to taste that sweet cream of yours," Greg said and singed her with his heated look.

"We all want a taste of that pretty little pussy, sweetness," Devon said from close behind her.

Keira felt hands go around her waist, and then they were on the fastenings of her jeans. They had her totally naked and on her back on the bed in seconds. Devon leaned over her and took her mouth. He slanted his lips over hers again and again, slipping his tongue between her lips and teeth until she was burning up from the inside out. She opened her eyes when she felt a mouth on her nipple and saw Jake suckling on the tip of her breast. God, they were going to kill her with pleasure.

Keira arched her hips up at the first touch of Greg's tongue to her clit and sobbed into Devon's mouth. Greg devoured her cunt like a man dying of thirst. He thrust his tongue into her pussy, deeper than she would have thought possible. He massaged her internal walls and had her on the edge of bliss so quickly she was lost. She writhed beneath them as they pleasured her to the edge of sanity. She mewled when she felt Greg thrust two fingers into the depths of her cunt, and he sucked her clit into his mouth. Her body trembled as she flew to the stars. She felt her cum gush from her pussy as her womb and pelvic-floor muscles contracted around the two digits buried in her body. The sound of Greg's growls as he ate her only pushed her higher. When the last spasm died, she was too exhausted to move. She didn't even care that her legs were wide open, displaying the most intimate part of her body.

"Your cunt is fucking beautiful, baby. I could eat that pussy for hours," Greg said as he sat up between her legs.

Keira didn't reply. She just groaned and covered her eyes with her arm. When she felt the bed dipping on all sides she removed her arm and snapped her eyelids open. She looked down her body to see Devon was now between her legs. He dove right on in and lapped at her cunt. *God, what are they doing to me? They're going to kill me.*

Keira didn't understand how her body could go from replete to an inferno so quickly, but she wasn't about to question it. She arched her hips up into Devon's mouth as he caged her now-sensitive clit between his teeth and laved her little pearl. Jake and Greg were now sucking on her nipples, and she felt the pleasure travel down her body to her pussy. She moaned as Devon slid two fingers into her sheath and twisted them. She felt him rub over a spot inside her which had her writhing. Her pelvic-floor muscles coiled, and she knew she was about to go over again. He pumped his fingers in and out of her, sliding over the sweet spot inside, and then he scraped his teeth lightly over her clit. She screamed, her whole body convulsing as the waves of pleasure swept over her. She felt her pussy gush and she heard Devon growl, and then he was slurping as he sucked her liquid into his mouth. Keira didn't know if she could take much more, but she knew when the bed dipped again Jake was about to eat her out.

Keira felt so weak with satiation she couldn't have moved if she wanted to. She mewled as Jake slipped his tongue through her drenched labia and tried to pull away. Her pussy was so sensitive from Greg and Devon's loving, she didn't think she could go another round. She looked down her body when Jake lifted his head, and the sight of his lips and chin glistening with her juices made her cunt clench, begging to be filled. She was turning into a nympho.

"Just relax, honey. I'll go nice and easy on you," Jake said and lowered his head again.

Keira groaned as Jake's tongue lightly touched on her clit. The soft, light touches were just what her sensitive clit needed, and she couldn't prevent her hips from bucking up into his mouth. Greg and Devon began to suckle her nipples again, but they had eased their intensity as well.

Hands caressed and smoothed over her chest and belly as Jake loved on her cunt gently. She sobbed as he slid two fingers into her pussy, thrust them in and out a couple of times then withdrew them. He massaged his wet fingers on the sensitive skin of her ass and pushed them into her anus. The buildup this time was much slower but no less intense. Actually, it was more intense than the last two times she had climaxed, and she didn't know if she could handle it. She reached out, determined to anchor herself as the storm grew in power. She wrapped her hands around the two large cocks close to her and began to pump them. She slid her hands up and down those hard shafts and was in awe that her fingers didn't touch. The now-familiar heaviness settled into her womb as her internal muscles contracted and released. The carnality of Jake sucking on her pussy while she gripped and pumped the cocks in her hands was too much.

She screamed as her body bowed off the bed, and she climaxed over and over again. Waves of pleasure rolled over her as she trembled uncontrollably. She felt her creamy liquid expulsing from her body. She was vaguely aware of Greg and Devon roaring, and then she felt their sperm shooting out of their pulsing cocks to cover her breasts and torso. Jake withdrew his mouth from her cunt and finger from her ass. She opened her eyes just in time to see him pump his cock once, twice, and then he roared as cum spewed from his dick onto her belly. She let go of the cocks in her hands, and her arms flopped down on the mattress as she tried to get her body to stop trembling. It was a lost cause. She was so weak from pleasure. She didn't think she'd ever be able to move again. She groaned when Devon picked her up and headed for the bathroom. She wasn't going to protest as her three men washed her body this time. She didn't have the energy.

Chapter Ten

Keira sighed with relief and stretched her tight muscles. She had just finished work and couldn't wait to see her mates.

Over the next few weeks Keira got into a routine, and she absolutely loved living with her men in the pack house. She was surrounded by people all the time, which she hadn't had since her parents had died. She was still worried about her brother finding her. But she was more worried that if he did, and she knew he would, her mates would be hurt. She spent every weekday working on the books at the club as Jake and Devon tended to the bar, and she really loved her work, but she was restless.

Keira had found out from her mates that her brother was involved with an illegal prostitution ring. To know that the brother she loved and thought she knew was kidnapping innocent women off the streets of Seattle and selling them to the mob was more than she could bear to comprehend. To think of the way she had tried to ingratiate herself to him and win his love like a good sister should, turned her stomach.

Jake had told her that everyone in the pack was on full alert and had been given a photo of her brother. So she knew if David was spotted in the town of Aztec they would have her locked away in the pack house for her own safety. Devon had been in contact with the police in Seattle, and they were apparently watching her brother and his cohorts. Now that she thought it over, she knew Devon would have told the police in Seattle where she was. That didn't sit well with her, but she didn't know why.

Keira rose from her chair behind the desk and walked out into the hall of the club. She made her way toward the bar, needing to see her mates. She sat on a stool and waited for Devon or Jake to come to her. She needed a drink and a break anyway, so she sat ogling her men. They were so sexy. Every time she laid eyes on them, her cunt would gush with desire and her heart would fill with emotion.

The door to the club opened, and she saw a tall, lithe man walk up to the bar. He was just over six feet, but he didn't have the muscle her men did. She felt his eyes slide over her, and she shivered with revulsion as his gray eyes connected with hers. She looked away and wanted to leave the room, but she wouldn't give him the satisfaction of knowing he gave her the willies.

He sat on the stool next to her and wanted to recoil as his scent enveloped her. She sighed with relief when her gentle but dominant giant stood opposite her.

"What can I get you, sweetness?" Devon asked.

Keira was grateful when he reached over and threaded his fingers through hers, a definite sign for the guy next to her that she was off the market.

"Can I have a sparkling water, please, honey?" Keira asked.

"You can have anything you like, darlin'," Devon replied and gave her a sexy wink.

He withdrew his hand from hers and went to get her drink.

"Excuse me, you obviously live here. I was wondering if you could tell me the best place to stay in town."

Keira turned to the man beside her as he spoke. She couldn't contain a shiver of fear traveling the length of her spine as she looked into his cold eyes. He thin lips had formed a smile, but that smile didn't reach his eyes.

"Here you go, sweet," Devon interrupted as he placed her fizzy water on the bar in front of her. "I couldn't help overhearing you're looking for somewhere to stay, Mr...."

"Yeah, sorry. The name's John Carmichael. And you are?"

"Devon Domain. The best place would be the motel down the end of this street. It's the only place in Aztec you can hire a room to spend the night. Are you on holiday?"

"No. Well, sort of. I'm here on business and depending on how that goes, I may stay a few days," John supplied. "You have a nice, quiet little town here. I can see the appeal after living in the city for so long."

"Where are you from?" Devon asked curiously.

"Washington State," John replied.

"I'm going to get back to work, Devon," Keira said and slid off her stool. She left the bar and shivered as she felt that man's eyes on her. She didn't like him one little bit. And the fact that he was from Washington had the hair on her nape prickling with warning.

Keira had just sat down at her desk when Jake walked into the office.

"Are you all right, honey?" Jake asked.

Keira stood up and met him in the middle of the office. She wrapped her arms around his waist and clung to him. His familiar scent and the warmth of his arms around her eased the tension from her muscles.

"John Carmichael gives me the creeps, Jake. I can't explain it, but I don't like him," Keira said, her voice muffled against his chest.

"Do you want me to take you home, honey?" Jake asked.

Keira clung to his neck as he scooped her up into his arms. He walked around behind her desk and sat down in the chair, holding her on his lap.

"No. I'm probably just being paranoid," Keira replied as she snuggled up with Jake.

"Maybe you are. Then maybe you're not. I always trust a gut instinct," Jake said, then growled as he nuzzled her neck with his nose and mouth. "You smell so good, honey. I can smell your cream from here."

"Oh my," Keira breathed out as Jake nibbled the length of her neck. She felt him pull her T-shirt from the waistband of her pants and then his hand slid up over her belly until he was cupping her breast. She moaned when he flicked her nipple with his thumb and his other hand worked at the button and zipper on her jeans.

Keira bucked her hips up when Jake slipped his hand beneath her panties and began to rub on her clit. Her pussy softened and leaked out her need, and she wanted to strip him down and impale herself on his hard cock. She shifted her hips and attacked his jeans with her hand. She moaned with appreciation as he helped her, and then he was in her hand. He was so soft and smooth, yet hard and hot. She slipped off his lap and knelt at his feet. She wrapped her hand around the base of his hard dick and began to slide her hand up and down his shaft. She leaned up and took the head of his cock into her mouth and sucked hard. She didn't get to taste as much as she liked, because Jake picked her up, his hands beneath her underarms, and he stripped her clothes from her body. He shoved his jeans down to his knees and pulled her onto his lap.

Keira grabbed hold of his cock again, aligned it with her needy pussy, and impaled herself. She moaned as her flesh enveloped his dick and held still a moment to savor the exquisite pleasure. She felt Jake's hands on her ass, and then rode him. She threw her head back and moaned as his shaft shuttled in and out her needy cunt. She obviously wasn't going fast enough for him because he held her slightly above him, her feet on the floor, straddling his thighs. He kept his hand on her ass and held her still as he pumped his hips in a fast, furious pace. He was so hard and deep, but she couldn't get enough. She clutched at his shoulders, digging her nails into his skin as her body wound tight.

Keira keened in the back of her throat as she went hurtling up and over the edge. She screamed as her walls clamped down on his cock and lowered her head to look into his eyes as he growled. She felt his cock jerk as he held still, buried in her depths, and shot his cum into her womb. Her legs trembled and she couldn't hold herself up anymore, even with Jake's help, so she collapsed down onto his lap. His still-hard rod went into her a little deeper and sent her over the edge once more.

Keira turned her head as the office door crashed open. The sight of Devon standing in the doorway looking ready to kill had her pussy clenching again.

"Fuck it, Jake. You could have warned me. I heard Keira screaming and thought she was hurt and in trouble," Devon stated, running a hand through his hair.

"You heard me?" Keira asked, feeling her cheeks heat with embarrassment.

"Sweetness, I'm a werewolf. Of course I heard you," Devon replied with a grin. "Do want some of this, baby?"

Keira looked down to where Devon was gripping his hard cock through his jeans, her cunt clenching with renewed fire.

"Oh yeah. Our honey wants some of that," Jake answered for her and eased his now-semihard cock from her pussy.

Jake stood up with Keira in his arms and handed her over to Devon. The sound of glass smashing and screams echoing through the air made all three of them move. Devon steadied Keira as her legs wobbled, and then he was out the door. Jake pulled his pants up and his shirt on and left, following his brother. Keira scrambled for her clothes and headed to the bathroom. She cleaned up quickly and then took off down the hall. She collided with a hard body and was about to apologize, but the apology died in her throat.

"Hello, Keira. You've led me on a merry chase, I must say. I didn't think you had it in you."

"David," Keira breathed and began to tremble. She backed away from him, hoping to get to the office or bathroom so she could lock herself in. She took two steps, and then he was on her. He grabbed a handful of hair, pulling her head back until her neck hurt. She lifted her hands, intent on getting him off her, but she stilled when she felt cold, hard metal poking into her stomach. She opened her mouth to scream, but she didn't get the chance.

"I wouldn't if I were you. You don't want me to have to shoot you now, do you, sister dear?"

"Why are you doing this, David? What have I ever done to you?" Keira whispered, afraid if she spoke too loudly Devon and Jake would come storming to her rescue and end up dead.

"You did nothing but exist, Keira. If it hadn't been for you, I would have had it all. Now, I can't go sharing any of that lovely money with you. That wasn't part of the plan at all." David chuckled.

"You won't get away with it, you know. The cops already know what you're doing," Keira said through clenched teeth.

"They might be aware of what I'm doing, sister dear, but they have no proof. Let's go," David demanded and yanked on her hair.

He had her out the back door to the club and in his black sedan before she could blink. She was in the driver's seat with a gun resting on her temple.

"Drive," David spat and pushed the gun harder into her head.

Chapter Eleven

"Where's Keira?" Devon asked once the bar had been cleared of people. He and Jake were standing in the parking lot out the front of the now-destroyed Aztec Club. Someone had thrown two homemade Molotov cocktails through the front window of the club. Glass and fire had exploded, and the club was in flames. He and Jake had made sure everyone was safely out of the burning building and had only now realized their mate wasn't amongst the people outside.

"Keira," Jake yelled and took off.

Devon sprang into action with his brother. They ignored the flames lapping around them and rushed to the back of the club.

"I can't even scent her with all the smoke and fire," Jake said as he rushed to the office.

Devon stopped in the doorway and backed up. He got a faint whiff of the unique perfume of Keira's scent, but it was being overshadowed by smoke. Devon stripped off his clothes and called to his wolf. He felt his muscles move and contort, and his bones cracked and popped as his skeleton compacted, and then he was standing on four paws. He sniffed the area thoroughly then threw his head up and howled in pain. Their mate had been taken. He growled low in his chest, his hackles rising, and he took off. He stopped in the parking lot where her scent ended and knew whoever had taken her was no longer on foot.

"Jake, Greg, Keira's been kidnapped. I'm going to stay in wolf form and see if I can track her. She's in a car with a male," Devon informed his brothers using their common mental link.

"I'll alert the pack," Greg growled.

"Jake, see if you can find Carmichael. I'd bet my last dollar he's involved in this," Devon said.

"I'm on it."

* * * *

Keira trembled so much she wondered how she kept the car on the road. She didn't know what to do, but she knew she had to do something. Her life depended on it.

"What are you going to do with me, David?" Keira asked and cursed the fact she heard her voice wobble.

"I haven't quite decided yet, sister. I could sell you off to the mob so they can use you as their own personal sex slave. I think you'd like that idea, wouldn't you? I would never have thought you were such a slut, Keira. I can't believe you of all people have been fucking three men. You're not as innocent as you portray, now are you? You're a little whore. No, maybe I should just arrange for you to have an accident like your folks. I wouldn't want you to enjoy yourself too much, now would I? What do you think, Keira? Should I sell you off to be used, or should I kill you?"

"Why, David? Why are you doing this? You have more money than you can poke a stick at. Why do you want more? Why did you have to kill my parents?" Keira asked with a sob.

"Oh you are still so naïve, sister. It's not just about the money. Of course the money was only half of it. I had already gone through my trust fund, and I needed more. I had to have control of all of it, Keira. They wouldn't have understood, and they wouldn't have just handed over more cash if I had told them I didn't have any left. I couldn't very well have taken yours. They would have been suspicious.

"It's about the power as well, dear sister. Do you know what it's like to have the bosses from the mob begging you to supply them with their little sex slaves? I have them in the palm of my hand. They come to me when they need something, Keira. They worship the ground I walk on. And you're a threat to everything because you know what I'm doing."

"You're crazy," Keira whispered through clenched teeth.

"Yes. I just might be at that," David replied and began to laugh.

The sound of his laughter grated on her nerves, but she tried to block it out. She needed to keep a cool head if she was to get out of this situation. She took note of landmarks as she drove and hoped when she had the chance to escape she would know the direction back to her mates. Keira saw the road sign indicating they were heading toward Farmington, and then she saw another sign showing the direction to the Four Corners airport.

"Slow down and take the next turn left," David snapped out.

When Keira saw another sign for the airport, her fear increased exponentially. She now knew David was going to fly her out of New Mexico, and there wasn't a thing she could do about it. She kept her eyes on the road, but she made sure to look for any opportunity for escape. She caught David's relaxed pose from her peripheral vision and knew he thought he had the upper hand. She needed to get out of here. If he got her onto a plane she would never be able to escape. She slowly but surely increased the speed at which they were traveling. She did it gradually, being careful so David wouldn't feel the pace of the car getting faster. She eased around the bend, thankful her parents had insisted she take intensive defensive driving lessons once she'd gotten her license at sixteen. She was more than capable of handling the car as they traveled around the long, sweeping bend. She saw another sign indicating the airport was only ten miles up the road and knew what she had to do.

She pushed her foot down on the accelerator a little more and knew when she felt the gun against her temple she had pushed too hard, too fast.

"Ease your foot off, Keira, or I'll shoot you now," David snapped.

Keira didn't ease off. She pushed down until her foot was flat to the floor.

"If you shoot me, you'll die, too. Is that what you want, David? Do you want to die beside me?" Keira asked maliciously, not caring if her brother pulled the trigger. She had the upper hand, and he knew it. She could kill them both with the flick of her wrist.

She saw David undo his seat belt, and then he leaned over her, trying to reach the keys and pull them from the ignition. Keira took her foot off the accelerator and slammed it down on the brake. The brakes locked up, and the tires screeched as they slid over the black tarmac of the road. David went slamming into the windscreen headfirst. The look of horror on his face as he went through the window would be forever etched into her mind.

She heard the sound of the gun going off as her brother flew past and out through the glass. She felt a searing pain in her shoulder and knew she had been shot. The bullet ripped through her flesh, and fiery pain emanated out from the bullet wound, up into her neck, and down her arm. She wrestled with the steering wheel as the back end of the car began to slide. The car spun on the road and she tried to circumvent the spin by taking her foot from the brake. She screamed with pain as she turned the steering wheel into the direction of the spin, using both hands to hold the wheel, but she just wasn't strong enough. She was in too much pain. She felt her conscious mind slipping as she battled the agony and the car.

Black spots formed before Keira's eyes, and she slipped into darkness as she lost the battle with the car and fainted.

* * * *

Jake couldn't find the man calling himself John Carmichael anywhere. He caught the man's scent mixed with oil and knew without a doubt that Carmichael had been involved in the explosion and destruction of the club. He knew Carmichael had been sent as a diversion so whoever had Keira could gain unimpeded access to her.

He howled out his frustration, his wolf taking over as his fear wrought through his system for his and his brothers' missing woman.

"Devon, are you still on her trail?" Jake asked his brother as he moved toward the truck he had driven to work that morning.

"Yes, they're headed toward Farmington," Devon replied.

"Fuck. Greg, where are you?" Jake asked.

"I'm already heading in your direction."

"Greg, have you passed the turnoff toward Farmington?" Jake asked.

"No, I can just see the sign now. I'll meet you there."

Jake ran for the truck and was on the road speeding for Farmington in moments. He pushed the accelerator pedal to the floor, fear for the safety of his mate making his heart beat fast. The knot of anguish in his gut was so big he felt his stomach churn. He breathed deeply and evenly, trying to get himself under control. The last thing he wanted was for his wolf to take over and for him to end up in his animal form with no control over the truck he was driving. The image burst through his mind, making him laugh, which helped ease some of his tension. How he could laugh at a moment like this was beyond him, but he was thankful, because he now had his emotions and beast back under control.

Jake was glad Greg would enter Farmington from the opposite side of town from him. There were only two ways in and out of the town besides the airport, so he knew if Keira were to come out the other side of the town, she would meet up with Greg.

Jake slowed the truck and stopped when he saw his brother trotting along the road in his wolf form. He leaned over and opened the door to let Devon in and watched as his brother changed back to his human form. Since they always carried a change of clothes wherever they went, Devon reached into the back and grabbed the clothes and began to dress.

"Go," Devon said.

Devon was just as eager as him to find their mate. He looked over at Devon as he drove, needing to know more information if possible.

"Did you recognize the scent of the male?" he asked.

"No. It could only be her brother or one of his colleagues. The scent was definitely human and not *were*," Devon growled. "How far are we from the turnoff?"

"Two miles," Jake pushed the accelerator flat to the floor.

Jake slowed the truck when he got to the turn, and hit the gas again after the bend. The black rubber marks on the road up ahead made his gut clench with fear. He slowed the truck and howled with pain when he saw the metal and rubber strewn about. The sight of a black car in a ditch on its roof was nearly his undoing. He stopped the truck, turned off the ignition, and was out of the driver's seat in seconds.

"The male is over there. He's dead. Looks like he went through the windscreen," Devon pointed out as he joined his brother.

"Fuck, she's still in there, Dev. We have to get her out," Jake said, hearing the anguish in his own voice.

Jake pulled on the driver's side door of the black sedan and wrenched it off the car. He threw it away and knelt down. The sight of Keira's bruised, bloody body and pale face made his wolf push against him. He reached in and checked for a pulse, his body slumping in relief when he felt it beating in her neck. He crawled into the car underneath her, wrapped his arm around her waist, and released the seat belt. He was careful that she didn't flop and fall into his arms. He eased her body down onto his and slowly crawled from the wreck. He was grateful when he felt Devon wrap his hands around his ankles and pull him free with Keira lying on top of him.

"I've called the paramedics," Devon stated as he helped Jake turn Keira onto her side.

Jake stilled on his knees above her when she moaned, but she didn't open her eyes. He could smell blood all over her and began to search for wounds. He let one of his claws elongate, and he sliced her shirt away. He found the gunshot wound on her shoulder and checked to see if the bullet was still in her body. There was an exit wound, and he was glad the bullet had gone right through her. He pulled his T-shirt off and tied it tightly around her, trying to stem the flow of blood. Once done, he checked the rest of her body. She had small cuts and abrasions as well as bruises. The biggest bruises were on her left shoulder and between her breasts from where the seatbelt had held her into the car. There was a large bruise and lump on her left temple, which he knew was the cause of her still being unconscious.

Jake turned his head when he heard tires squealing on the asphalt and looked up to see Greg pulling up in his truck. His brother ran over to them and knelt down at Keira's side. He looked up into Greg's gaze and saw moisture in his eyes.

"She's alive. The paramedics are on their way," Jake stated, trying to ease his brother's anguish.

Jake watched as Greg threw his head back and howled. The sound had chills racing up and down his own spine because he had sounded just like his brother a bit earlier. Fur erupted on Greg's arms, and he knew his brother was out of control. He had to get Greg settled because he could hear the sirens in the distance. The last thing they needed was for the humans to find out about their kind. He grabbed his brother by the shoulders and shook him.

"You can't do this, Greg. You have to keep it together for Keira," Jake said. "Come on, man, the paramedics will be here any moment."

Jake watched as his oldest brother breathed heavily, struggling with his wolf. He saw when his brother won the battle against his wolf. His brother's eyes changed from gold to brown, and his fur receded back under his skin. He was just in time.

The paramedics were at their side moments later. The two men checked Keira over and then slid a large needle into the back of her hand, hooking her up to a saline solution. They slid a backboard beneath her and then transferred her to the mobile stretcher. They wheeled her to the back of the ambulance and slid her in.

Chapter Twelve

Devon paced the waiting room outside the emergency theater. They had wheeled Keira away behind those double doors, and he had been pacing impatiently ever since. The sight of her pale, bruised face as she had disappeared from his view made his heart clench with fear and sorrow. He hoped to never see his mate looking so weak and fragile again. He had been waiting for over two hours now, and he wanted to go bursting through those doors and get some answers. He looked up and down the hallway when he scented his brothers. He could see the anxiety on Greg's and Jake's faces and wanted to be able to tell them some news, but he didn't know anything himself. Just as they got to his side, the double doors to the theater opened to admit a small woman who didn't look old enough to be practicing medicine.

"Are you with Keira O'Lachlan?" the small woman asked.

"Yes. How is she?" Devon asked.

"She is fine. She has remarkable healing capabilities. The gunshot wound has closed and is healing rapidly. Would you know the reason for this miracle?"

Devon wasn't sure how to answer. He looked at his brothers and back to the young doctor again. Greg move forward from the corner of his eye until he stood in front of the woman.

"If I tell you, you will have to keep it a secret. The last thing we need is the government or the medical profession coming after us," Greg replied.

"How about you all follow me to my office? I'm Dr. Charity Stoner," Dr. Stoner said.

"Keira was shot in the shoulder and even though the bullet went straight through there was a lot of tissue and ligament damage. The bleeding has stopped and the arteries and veins have closed. I disinfected her shoulder and gave her a shot of antibiotics to stave off infection, but from what you have told me I don't think we have anything to worry about. She lost quite a bit of blood, but I didn't need to transfuse her. She has a large contusion on her left temple, which is my biggest worry. She hasn't regained consciousness, and the longer she stays out the more there is to worry over. If she isn't awake within the next hour, I will have to inject dye into her body and have an MRI scan done on her brain. If her brain is swollen and bruised it could mean she has brain damage, but we won't know for sure until she's awake."

"Fuck it. If that bastard wasn't already dead, I'd kill him myself." Jake growled.

"I'd like to know what happened to Keira if you have the time to explain," Dr. Stoner said.

Dr. Stoner's pager beeped, and she tilted it up then smiled at them.

"Keira has just regained consciousness," Dr. Stoner said. "I'm sure you'd like to see her."

Devon and his brothers followed Dr. Stoner from her office down the corridor and into a curtained-off cubicle. The sight of their mate trying to reach for a cup of water was the best thing Devon had seen all day. He rushed over to the table and picked up the cup. He sat on the side of the bed, slid an arm beneath her shoulders, and supported her weight as he held the cup to her lips. She took a few sips, and then he helped to ease her back down to the pillows.

"Keira, I'm glad to see you awake. I'm Dr. Charity Stoner and have been looking after you. Do you remember what happened?"

"David, he kidnapped me at gunpoint. He was taking me to the airport outside of Farmington. I crashed the car," Keira whispered.

Devon saw the tears in Keira's eyes, and from the glazed look and sluggish pupils, he knew she had to have one hell of a headache. He wrapped her in his arms and kissed the top of her head.

"You're safe now, sweetness. He won't be bothering you anymore," Devon stated, his throat tight with emotion.

"He's dead, isn't he? I killed my own brother," Keira whispered and began to cry. The sound of her sniffling and sobbing had moisture gathering in Devon's eyes. He looked to his brothers and saw they were in the same condition as he was.

"I'll leave you to comfort your mate. I still want to hear what happened from you all one day real soon," Dr. Stoner said to Devon and his brothers and then left the room. She popped her head back around the curtain a moment later and smiled. "Keira is going to be just fine."

Devon closed his eyes and inhaled Keira's familiar sweet scent as he picked her up into his arms and rocked her as she cried. Once she was done with her tears, she slumped down against him and drifted off to sleep. He would tell her when she was awake later that she didn't have an option about David. It had been a choice of her brother or her, and he was glad she had chosen to keep herself alive.

Devon and his brothers sat at Keira's bedside for the next twenty-four hours. She drifted in and out of sleep as the swelling on her brain slowly lessened. They were eager to get her home and back in their bed where she belonged, and Dr. Stoner had said they would be able to take her home today.

By the time Keira woke, the sun streamed in the windows. Devon had been glad his Alphas and Michelle had popped in for a visit last night to see how Keira was, and he was thankful Michelle had brought some of Keira's clothes with her. He was eager to get out into the fresh air and away from the smells of the vomit and the clinical disinfectant used in the hospital.

Keira was sitting up now, and she had a healthy rosy glow back in her cheeks. The bruise and knot on her temple had diminished, but he could still see by her eyes she was in a little pain. When she flung the cotton blanket aside and moved her legs over the edge of her bed, he and his brothers were at her side in an instant.

"What are you doing, sweetness?" Devon asked as he took hold of her hand.

"I need to use the bathroom and then I am going to shower," Keira replied.

"Let me help you, baby," Greg stated as he scooped her up into his arms.

"No. Put me down, Greg. I can do this myself."

"I know you can, Keira. Just humor me, okay? I need to feel you in my arms and take care of you for a bit," Greg stated.

Devon bit back a smile as he heard Keira sigh with resignation. He knew their mate was itching to give Greg a mouthful, but she closed her mouth, her lips in a thin line as she held her tongue. Yep, their little mate was going to be just fine.

* * * *

Devon was in the backseat of Greg's truck with Keira. He had her snuggled up against his side and wasn't about to let her pull away anytime soon. To have her in his arms, her scent in his nostrils, and the heat of her body against his after such a scare was pure heaven. He knew his brothers wanted to be in the back with their mate as well, because Greg kept glancing at her from the rearview mirror and Jake kept turning around to check on her.

He had his arm wrapped around her shoulders, her head was resting on his chest, and she was sound asleep. No matter what she said, Keira still wasn't fully recovered from her ordeal. As soon as they got her home, he was going to carry her up to their suite of rooms and tuck her into bed so she could rest. Keira stirred when Greg slowed the truck and pulled into the driveway of the pack house. She lifted her head from his chest with a yawn and stretched.

"Are we home already?" Keira asked.

"Yeah, sweetness. How do you feel?" Devon asked.

"Tired. I would love a bath though."

"You can have anything you want, baby. We'll have you settled in no time," Greg called from the front.

"I just need a bath. My muscles are still a little sore," Keira stated.

"We'll give you a massage after your bath. That should help relieve some of the soreness," Jake said.

"You don't have to…" Keira began.

"We know we don't have to, sweetheart, we want to. We like taking care of you. It makes us feel good," Devon said with a gentle smile.

"Well, in that case, I would love a massage," Keira replied.

Devon gave Keira another hug and scooped her up onto his lap as Greg pulled the car into the carport. He was out of the truck and on his way through the door to the house before she could protest.

"You don't have to carry me," Keira protested halfheartedly, wrapping her arms around his neck.

"I like carrying you," Devon replied and continued right on up the stairs to their rooms and into the bathroom, his brothers following behind.

Devon sat her on his lap while Greg ran the bath, and he began removing her clothes with the help of his brothers. When Keira was naked, Devon handed her over to Greg and began to strip off his clothes. He climbed into the tub and took her back into his arms, settling down in the hot water while his brothers removed their clothes. He picked up some bath gel, squirted it onto a cloth, and began to wash his mate. The sound of her sighs as he ran the cloth over her body made his dick jump and twitch with interest, and even though he couldn't control his unruly cock around his mate, he knew she wasn't up to any loving. She was still recovering.

Devon's brothers slipped into the water, and they surrounded Keira. They each washed her, needing to touch her and to reaffirm to themselves and their wolves that their mate was safe and well. Once they were done, Jake climbed from the tub first and dried off. He slipped from the room carrying a large towel and a bottle of massage oil. He was back in moments, and Devon passed Keira over to him as he and Greg got out to dry off, too.

Once he was done, he helped Jake finish patting Keira dry and stepped back as Jake lifted her into his arms and carried her to the bedroom. He laid her down on her belly on the strategically placed towel and straddled her thighs.

Jake passed the bottle of oil to Devon who poured some of the oil into his own palms and handed it off to Greg. Devon began to massage her arms and shoulders, while Jake massaged her back and Greg her legs. The sounds coming from Keira made his balls ache and his cock elongate, and he could see his brothers were in the same condition. He massaged and kneaded her tight muscles until they were soft and supple beneath his hands and fingers. The scent of her musky arousal permeated the air, and Devon wanted to turn her over and bury himself balls-deep into her tight, wet pussy.

"Let's turn you over, sweetheart," Devon said in a rumbling voice.

He and his brothers gently turned Keira on to her back, collected more oil, and began to smooth their hands over her body. He massaged, caressed, and soothed along with his brothers until their mate was arching up into their hands. Greg shifted from her legs over to her other side, and Jake moved his body between her now-spread legs.

Devon leaned down and began to nibble at her lips. Jake bent over her and took one of her nipples into his mouth, and Greg settled between her legs to lap at her pussy. He and his brothers held her down gently so Keira wouldn't hurt any of her aching muscles and concentrated on making her feel good. Devon ended the kiss and looked down to watch Greg, which had saliva pooling in his mouth.

He knew what that sweet little pussy tasted like and was hankering for his own taste. Instead he swallowed, leaned over Keira from her side and moved to nibble on her other breast. The mewling sound his mate made had his cock so hard it jerked with every beat of his heart. He was going to have to jack off in the shower after they had pleasured Keira and let her rest. He looked down her body as he suckled on her tit and saw his brother pumping his fingers in and out of Keira's cunt while sucking her little nub into his mouth.

She tried to buck as she screamed, but he and his brothers held her still while she rode out her release. When the last quiver had died, Devon kissed her on the lips and got up. He needed to masturbate in the worst way, and he intended to do just that. The last thing he wanted was to hurt Keira by making love to her. His mate sighed one last time and fell asleep with a smile on her face. He watched as Jake and Greg covered her with a quilt, and then they, too, headed for the shower.

Devon was deeply in love with Keira and wanted to spend the rest of his life by her side. He hoped he never had to see her hurt or in danger again. He could just imagine how she would look with her belly swollen as she nurtured their child in her womb.

Chapter Thirteen

Keira breathed in the perfume of jasmine and sage as she stepped out onto the back patio. She loved the scents of the night as the sun set with a blaze of glory. She looked back over her shoulder as Michelle joined her outside.

"I need some air," Keira stated.

"I could use some myself," Michelle replied and followed behind Keira.

She and Michelle had become fast friends, and they were often in the monstrous living room sitting on the sofa, chatting as they drank a glass of wine. Keira knew Michelle could tell she still felt guilty over the death of her brother, but the other woman, as well as her mates, had tried to ease her burden by telling her she had done the only thing possible at the time. And even though she knew that was true, she still woke up some nights drenched in sweat after reliving that horrible day. Her mates were solicitous to the point of aggravating, and they wouldn't let her out of their sight. She knew it was because not all of her brother's cohorts had been captured by the police, but she was getting tired of them being around her twenty-four-seven. Michelle's mates were treating her the same way. Since they had just found out she was pregnant with the Alphas' pup, Michelle had changed her glass of wine for fruit juice, and she would still sit and chat with Keira most nights. That is, if she wasn't rushed off to the bedroom by her three Alpha mates.

"How are you feeling?" Keira asked curiously.

"Not so bad," Michelle replied. "I get a little queasy in the mornings, but so far that's all, thank God. I have a checkup in two weeks. The expansion to the doctor's office should be finished by then."

"When Jonah makes a decision he doesn't do things by halves. I can't believe he has expanded the room Blayk uses to add an operating theater and all the necessary equipment," Keira said.

"He takes his responsibility of lead Alpha very seriously. The pack and its members mean everything to him and his brothers. To me as well, now. It's hard to explain. When he and his brothers claimed me it was like each and every pack member was a special part of my family. I can feel everyone here," Michelle said, placing a hand over her heart. "Including you. You're like the sister I never had."

"Oh," Keira responded, tears of emotion filling her eyes. "Stop that right now or you'll have me crying."

"Don't start. Now that I'm pregnant, my emotions are all over the place," Michelle replied with a watery smile and a sniff.

Keira followed as Michelle stepped off the patio, and they began to wander the gardens. They were so beautiful and peaceful. Keira could have spent hours traversing the paths and sniffing the blooms. They stopped before a beautiful fountain and listened as the water trickled from the hands of the image of the Greek goddess Gaea, the mother of earth. Keira had always thought the fountain of Gaea was a fitting tribute for werewolves, considering she was the daughter of Chaos and had supposedly born the Titans and some of the Cyclopes.

Keira turned toward Michelle as her queen sat down on the bench near the fountain. She caught movement from the corner of her eye and looked over to her left. The sight of a strange man pointing a gun at Michelle made fear shudder through her body.

She had never seen him before and knew Michelle didn't know he was there. She knew Michelle was pregnant with her mates' baby and she couldn't let her new friend or her unborn child get hurt. She thought she may have yelled a warning but couldn't be sure. She felt as if she were moving in slow motion.

She spun on her heel and felt the muscles in her thighs contract. Her heart was pounding in her ears, and she could hear nothing else. She was breathing heavily as adrenaline flowed through her in response to the danger. Her body was in the flight-or-fight mode.

Keira reacting without thinking. She leapt the distance between them and knocked Michelle to the ground. The sound of the gun exploding was so loud in the still night. The report seemed to echo on and on and on. Keira cried out as pain radiated into her side and knew she had taken a bullet. She felt white-hot fire slicing in between her ribs, and she was having trouble breathing. She could hear Michelle sobbing beneath her and hoped she hadn't hurt her or her baby. She wanted to get up, to take her weight off of Michelle, but she couldn't seem to move.

The growls and howls nearby grew dimmer and dimmer. Her own heartbeat and breathing were so loud in her ears. She couldn't hear anything else. She slipped away to float on a cloud of light where there was no pain, only peace and tranquility. She could hear voices calling to her from a place far away and knew she should know the owners of those voices, but she couldn't concentrate long enough to place them. The light seemed to get brighter, and she had to squint to be able to perceive the little she could. She could see shapes moving toward her but couldn't ascertain who they were.

Keira must have closed her eyes, because when she opened them, her mom and dad were standing before her.

"Mom, Dad, what are you doing here?" Keira asked with confusion.

"It's not your time, Keira. You must go back," her mom said.

"I'm so tired, Mom. I just want to sleep."

"No, Keira." Her dad spoke up. "You must fight. You can't give up. You have three very special men who love and need you. You will go back, daughter. Everything is done for a purpose. You must remember that."

"I don't know if I have the strength to fight anymore," Keira sobbed.

"You have more strength than you'll ever know," Keira's mom said with a smile. "Do not worry over David. It was not your fault. He only has himself to blame. You tried so hard, baby. We are so proud of you. We will always be watching over you, Keira. Never forget that. You are going to be so strong. There is a greater purpose at work here. Embrace your new life, daughter. Don't let the rules of society impinge on the love you have for those three men. Take what they give you and hold on tight. It was meant to be. We love you, Keira."

"Don't go. Stay with me! I love you," Keira called out as her parents began to fade back into the light. She tried to keep her eyes open, but she was so tired. Her eyelids slid closed, and she drifted away.

* * * *

Greg, along with his brothers and Alphas, launched himself into the air at the sound of gunshot fire. They had changed from man to beast in the blink of an eye, before their four paws landed back on the floor. He was outside in a flash and pounced on the man who was standing over his mate and queen. He leaped up and ripped his throat out before the man could raise the gun at him. The stranger hit the ground moments after his death. Greg was at his mate's side an instant later, once more in his human form.

The sight of his mate lying on the path with blood pouring from her side sent tears coursing down his cheeks. His Alphas' queen was lying beneath Keira, her face white with shock. His Alphas and his brothers helped to lift his Keira from Michelle, and Greg placed his hands over her rib cage where the bullet had entered. In moments his hands were covered with her blood. He pushed down hard, trying to stem the flow, but it didn't seem to help. He could hear how slow and erratic Keira's heartbeat was and knew they were about to lose her.

He looked up at his Alpha Jonah when he felt the man place his hand on his shoulder.

"You have to turn her, Greg. It's the only chance she has at surviving," Jonah stated quietly.

"I can't, it will kill her," Greg cried with anguish.

"She's dead if you don't try. I can feel her slipping away just as you can," Jonah said.

"I don't know if I can. The thought of ripping into her flesh sickens me. It goes against everything a mate does to protect his woman," Greg said through his tears.

"Let me do it," Chris Friess, Jonah's cousin and Beta said, stepping forward. Greg saw him look to Jonah, who gave a nod in acquiescence. "Get a hold of Greg and his brothers. I don't want them trying to rip my throat out."

Greg resisted being pulled away from Keira, but he was dragged back several feet. He and his brothers had four men apiece holding them back. He knew this was the only way Keira had a chance of survival, but he knew what came next. He could feel his beast pushing against him for dominance and tried to keep control. He watched as Chris transformed into his wolf, and then he ravaged his woman violently. The sound of Chris's snarls as he tore at Keira's stomach and organs made fur erupt out of his skin, claws piercing through his fingertips, and his face contorting. He and his brothers howled as their mate convulsed and was ripped apart. He was aware of Chris backing away from his mate and changing back to his human form, but the sight of Blayk working on Keira's body transfixed him. He pumped her chest and breathed for her, keeping her alive with his own breath.

Blayk didn't let up once on Keira. Not when his Alphas helped to transfer her to a portable stretcher, or while they wheeled his mate to the doctor's office at the back of the house. Greg and his brothers followed. His body felt as if it were on automatic. He was aware of everything around him, but it all seemed so surreal.

Greg stood at the back of the room with Jake and Devon, willing their mate to breathe on her own. An oxygen mask was placed over Keira's mouth and nose, while Blayk kept her heart pumping. Blayk told his brothers Chris and James to place the heart monitor tags on Keira's chest. His woman was linked up to the ECG moments later, and her slow, erratic heartbeat was the most beautiful sound he'd ever heard.

Blayk hooked his mate up to a drip, and then he worked on her injuries. The sight of her stomach ripped to shreds and the jagged bullet hole made his wolf push against him again, but he was more in control now that Chris had finished tearing his mate apart. Blayk pulled the bullet from Keira's side and began washing her wounds with saline and disinfectant. Greg knew there was no need to do anything more. If the attack on his mate from his cousin had taken, Keira's transformation into a werewolf had already begun. Now it was just a waiting game.

Blayk collected a couple of bags of blood and hooked his mate up to begin the transfusion. Greg knew that the blood would be from him and his brothers. All the pack members gave blood regularly in case of any grievous wounds to the wolves of the pack. By giving Keira blood from him, Jake, and Devon she would have a better chance of survival since their DNA was already in her system.

His knees buckled as the heart monitor went crazy. His mate's heart was beating so fast and erratically that he was scared it was the end. He rushed over to her side and took her hand in his own. Her body began shaking, and then she convulsed on the table. He helped Blayk hold his mate down so she wouldn't fall from the bed. She had foam frothing around her mouth, and her eyes snapped open. She opened her mouth and screamed. The sound was so full of pain. He felt tears running down his cheeks again. When he looked up he saw Jake and Devon at Keira's side, and they each touched her anywhere they could. Greg heard the sound of his own tortured voice from a distance, pleading with his mate to fight and live. Her body stopped mid convulsion, and she slumped back onto the bed. She was so quiet and still. Her back no longer bowed. He laid his head down next to Keira's and wept.

The sound of the steady breathing and the now-steady heartbeat blipping on the monitor began to penetrate his senses. He lifted his head from the bed, not caring that everyone in the room could see the tears he'd shed for the woman he loved. He saw his brothers' eyes and cheeks were just as wet as his.

Greg looked over to Blayk and saw his cousin smiling. Renewed hope surged into him, filling his empty heart with joy, but he gave Blayk a questioning look.

"She's not out of the woods yet. The next few hours will be the most critical, but I think the change has taken. Her heartbeat is stronger and she's resting peacefully. The wounds should close up in the next hour, and then she'll sleep a deep, healing sleep," Blayk explained.

Greg was too choked up to speak, so he gave his cousin a nod of thanks. He looked to Chris, who now stood at the back of the room, away from his mate. The man looked really worried as Greg stood up and walked toward him. He reached out and thumped Chris on the back.

"Thank you. Thank you for saving my mate," Greg said, his voice sounding emotional even to his own ears. His cousin gave him a nod, smiled, and thumped him in return. He watched as Chris left the room without a backward glance.

Greg sat at Keira's bedside without moving for the next four hours, his brothers right beside him. He watched as Blayk checked Keira's vital signs every hour on the hour. He gave her two more pints of blood, and his mate rested peacefully. Her wounds had closed, and if he hadn't seen them with his own eyes, he would never have known they existed.

Blayk had tried to get Greg and his brothers to leave the room to rest, but there was no way in hell he was leaving until he knew for sure his mate was out of the woods. Pack members were in and out of the room checking on him, his brothers, and his mate all throughout the long night. Angie the housekeeper kept sending a different person out with food and drink for him, his brothers, and Blayk. He wasn't interested in the food, but the coffee helped to keep him alert, especially in the early hours of the morning. His eyelids were so heavy and his eyes so sore from crying earlier that he ended up closing them for a moment, his head resting on the side of the bed, his cheek against the back of Keira's hand.

The next thing he knew was the light touch of fingers running through his hair. He opened his eyes and looked up to see Keira looking at him from beneath lowered lashes. She smiled at him as her eyes closed once more, the sound of her sweet voice filling him with love and joy.

"I love you," Keira whispered, and then she was sound asleep.

Chapter Fourteen

Keira gained strength steadily over the next few days. She was released from the medical room and allowed back into the house and her mates' bed, but only if she rested. Of course she agreed. She felt so much stronger than she had before and knew she had been changed into a werewolf. She had found out from her mates the stranger who had tried to shoot Michelle had been one of David's cronies out to get Keira but aimed for the wrong woman. Fate had stepped in, and Keira had ended up shot anyway. She had nearly died, and the only way for her mates to keep her by their side had been to change her.

Michelle visited her often and had told her how Chris had ripped into her stomach and organs to begin the change. The DNA of a werewolf was like a virus to a normal human being and had to be deeply embedded into the body to take. The only way the Friess Pack members had heard of a change ever taking was by violently ripping deep enough into the flesh so the virus could begin to mutate.

Keira thanked God she hadn't been aware of any of that. The thought of the pain she would have endured if she had been conscious still made her feel ill.

Greg, Jake, and Devon were with her nearly all the time. They took shifts to keep her occupied by playing games of cards, checkers, and chess with her. Even Jonah, Mikhail, and Brock visited her regularly. They had each thanked her for saving their mate's and unborn child's lives.

Keira was getting sick and tired of being cooped up in the same room night and day and, after the fourth day of convalescence, decided she'd had enough. She decided she was going to have her lunch downstairs with the rest of the pack. She missed the having lots of people around her.

"What the hell are you doing out of bed? God, Keira you shouldn't be up," Greg stated vehemently.

"Oh, yes, I should. I feel fine. In fact I've never felt better. I need to get out of that room, Greg. I'll go crazy if I have to spend another minute in there," Keira replied.

"Okay. But if I see any signs of you getting tired you'll be back in that bed before you can blink," Greg stated quietly.

"Deal. Let's go," Keira said with a smile and headed downstairs, Greg on her heels.

Keira walked into the dining room and took her seat beside Jake. Devon jumped up from his seat and moved over to where Greg usually sat. He and Jake glared at her.

"What the fuck are you doing down here, Keira?" Devon snapped.

"What does it look like I'm doing? I'm going to eat lunch," Keira replied.

"Don't you get sassy with me, little girl. You should be in bed resting," Devon grumbled.

Keira had had enough of being looked after. She glanced down the table to see Blayk smiling at her as he watched Jake and Devon scowling at her.

"Blayk, you gave me the all clear, right?" Keira asked loud enough for everyone in the room to hear.

"Yes, Keira. You're right as rain. I'd say you're even better than before," Blayk replied with a smile and a wink.

"Thank you," Keira said to Blayk and turned back to Devon and Jake, who were now eyeing her surreptitiously. "I'm hungry. Can you please pass the steak?"

Keira sat back after eating and wondered where she put all the food she had consumed. She felt like she'd made an absolute pig of herself and looked up to see her mates smiling at her. She felt her cheeks heat with embarrassment and lowered her eyes to her plate, but she could still feel their eyes on her. She finally looked up at them and glared.

"What?"

"Nothing, baby. It's just so good to see you up and about," Greg answered from beside Devon.

"If I could have everyone's attention," Jonah said as he stood up at the end of the table.

Keira turned to face Jonah and listen to what he had to say.

"Tonight is a full moon and the pack will run as usual. But tonight has taken on a special celebration as we welcome our newly formed wolf sister into our fold.

"Keira, you have the gratitude of my brothers, my mate, and myself. If it wasn't for you, my mate would most certainly not be alive. Your unselfish act of throwing yourself in front of a bullet meant for our mate has ingratiated you into our hearts. If there is ever anything you want or need you only have to come to me and it will be yours without question. There will be a special dinner in honor of you tonight and in celebration of your first change to your wolf. The run will begin at nine o'clock. Thank you from the bottom of my heart," Jonah said and raised his glass to her in a toast.

Keira felt tears flowing down her cheeks when every pack member in the room stood and toasted her for something she hadn't even thought about doing. She felt her cheeks heat and knew she was bright red. She lowered her eyes amidst the wolf howls, catcalls, and accolades and whispered her thanks, knowing that the people would hear her with their enhanced hearing. When they all sat down and began to talk amongst themselves, Keira was relieved. She hated being the center of attention.

"Baby, you look tired. Why don't you go and have a nap so you're not too tired to run tonight?" Greg said, leaning across Devon to speak to her.

Keira looked at Greg with disbelief. Now that she knew she would run as a wolf for the first time, she was full of nervous energy. She was worried changing forms would hurt and wasn't really looking forward to the experience.

"I'm fine," Keira replied.

"No, you're not, honey," Jake whispered in her ear. "I can smell your fear. Come on, let's go."

Keira eyed Jake warily as he stood and pulled her up from her chair. Greg and Devon stood as well. They pulled her from the dining room and back up the stairs to their rooms.

"What are you scared of, baby?" Greg asked from near her feet.

"Does it hurt? The change, I mean. It sounds so painful. Michelle told me all about what she's seen when her mates change," Keira whispered.

"The first time, your bones ache a little as they transform. It's not unlike growing pains. You'll handle it just fine, baby," Greg said.

"I'm worried I'll make a fool of myself. I hate any sort of pain and I don't want to embarrass you by crying."

"Honey, you are the bravest person I have ever met. If you can throw yourself in front of a bullet and then go through the transformation of becoming a werewolf without making a sound, the change from human to wolf will be a piece of cake. Now lie back and let us help you to relax," Jake said, pushing gently on her shoulder.

They had her stripped and lying naked on the bed moments later.

She watched as they began to remove their clothes and felt her breath hitch as they revealed their muscular bodies to her hungry gaze. The sight of their muscles rippling and their erections swaying and bobbing as they moved made her pussy clench with desire. She didn't know what she'd done to deserve three sexy men in her life as her husbands, her mates, but she wasn't going to question their presence. They climbed onto the bed and sighed as they surrounded her with their masculine scents and heat.

Keira lay back and sighed as her mates' hands began to caress over her naked skin. She arched up into their touch and closed her eyes, giving herself over into their care. Hands smoothed down, massaging tight muscles as they travelled the length of her body. She couldn't prevent crying out with need as warm, wet mouths enveloped her aching nipples. She spread her legs wide when large, callused palms smoothed up her inner thighs, begging for them to touch her where she needed it most.

She sifted her fingers through Jake's and Devon's hair, holding them to her breasts, and they suckled, laved, and nibbled on the hard peaks. She mewled in the back of her throat when Greg took his first lick of her wet pussy after so long without. She needed them so badly. It had been too long since they had loved her. She felt restless and itching, like something was crawling under her skin. She cried out when Greg thrust his fingers into her needy cunt and bucked her hips up to his mouth. She growled with frustration when she heard him chuckle against her flesh, the vibrations going deep into her womb. He teased around her sensitive nub, licking around the sides, over the top and bottom of her clit, but not once did he touch her there with his tongue.

"Fuck me, damn it. Lick my clit and fuck me." Keira growled. She froze at the animalistic growl coming from her own mouth and whimpered with fear.

"Shh, baby. It's all right. Don't be scared. Your wolf is trying to take over. Don't fight me, baby, just relax. I'll take good care of you, I promise," Greg said in a soothing voice.

Keira took a deep breath and tried to relax her taut muscles. She was rewarded when Greg took her clit into her mouth and sucked on the sensitive little bud firmly, as he thrust his fingers in and out of her pussy. She screamed as he sent her over the edge into nirvana. She opened her eyes to see her three mates staring at her.

"You are so beautiful, Keira. I love you so much," Greg said as he moved up between her thighs.

"I love you, too. I love you all more than I can bear," Keira replied, looking each of her men in the eye as tears of joy spilled over her cheeks.

"I love you, honey," Jake stated.

"I love you, too, sweetness," Devon replied and took her mouth beneath his.

Keira opened her mouth for Devon and moaned as he swept the interior with his tongue. He tasted every inch he could reach and had her desire heating up once more. She felt Jake suck on her nipple, and then she arched her hips when she felt Greg's cock at her pussy. She tried to get him inside her body, but he grabbed hold of her hips and kept her still. She sobbed into Devon's mouth and sucked on his tongue as she arched up. She panted for breath when Devon weaned his mouth from hers.

Keira looked down her body and stared into Greg's brown eyes. He slowly worked the head of his erection into her wet cunt, and she moaned as he filled her. She had never felt so loved and cherished as she did right then. The emotional connection she had with these three men was so strong. She couldn't even begin to describe it with words. She pushed her hips at Greg and groaned as he slid into her the rest of the way, his balls touching the cheeks of her ass.

Keira cried out when Jake and Devon moved away from her breasts, and then she was sitting up on Greg's lap, impaled on his hard cock. She reached out, taking his face between the palms of her hands, and pulled his mouth down to hers. She kissed him, putting all the love and emotion in to the act. Letting him know he was so very special to her. When the need to breathe took over, she pulled her mouth from his and held his eyes to hers. She heard the sound of a top popping and knew she was going to be loved by all her men at the same time.

Keira smiled when Greg groaned, her inner walls clamping down on his dick in anticipation. She mewled when she felt the cold, gel-coated fingers massaging her ass and concentrated on relaxing her muscles. The sensation of two large digits thrusting in and out of her asshole had her on the brink of climaxing again, those fingers scissoring and massaging as they stretched her tight muscles. The appendages withdrew, and then she felt the large blunt head of a cock pushing into her ass. She shivered as Devon's warm, moist breath caressed her ear.

"Push back against me, sweetheart," Devon whispered. "Oh, fuck yeah, Keira. Your ass is so tight. You feel so good wrapped around my cock. That's it, sweetness. You're doing great. Can you feel me, Keira? Can you feel my dick sliding into your ass?"

"Yes. Oh God. You're so big, Devon. You hurt me so good," Keira moaned.

Keira squeezed her eyes shut, overwhelmed by the pleasure of having two cocks in her body at the same time. She was stuffed so full. But something was missing. She still needed more. She turned her head, searching, and found just whom and what she was looking for.

Keira opened her mouth wide and licked over the top of Jake's cock. Her desire went up to the next level at the sound of his groan. She opened her mouth wide and sucked him into her depths until the tip of his erection touched the back of her throat. The taste of his salty-sweet pre-cum made her crave more. She reached over, wrapped her hand around the base of his cock, and began to pump her hand as she bobbed her head. She made sure to lick the sensitive underside of his cock with her tongue as she drew back up over his dick. The growls and moans he made were music to her ears. She picked up the pace until she was in a nice, steady rhythm, which she knew wouldn't take long to send him over the edge.

"Yeah, honey. That's it. Suck my cock. Your mouth is so sweet, Keira. I could spend hours fucking your sweet little mouth," Jake groaned out.

Keira couldn't answer, so she just moaned, which seemed to turn Jake on even more. He grabbed a handful of her hair, held her head steady, and began to rock his hips, sliding his cock in and out of her mouth.

Greg and Devon began to pump their hips at the same time, gliding their cocks in and out of her ass and cunt. The friction of two cocks shafting her holes had her back on the edge in seconds. She was full of cock one moment and nearly empty the next. There was a burning, pinching pain in her ass, since Devon's cock was such a monster, but the slight pain only seemed to enhance her pleasure. As she sucked on Jake, she began to rock her hips back and forth, needing the movement to help send her over into bliss. Her movement must have been a sign to her men, because they let go of their control and began to slam up against her body. Their cocks were now moving so fast she couldn't keep up the pace, so she held still and let them move her however they desired.

Keira felt her womb becoming heavy with desire as fluid seeped from her cunt. The warm tingles emanated out from her belly, over her clit, deep into her pussy, and down her legs. The coils gathered tighter and tighter, and she knew she was about to climax. She heard Jake roar out with pleasure, and she gulped down his cum, not willing to lose a drop. She licked him clean and released him with an audible pop. She threw her head back and cried out as those coils froze in motion then snapped and sent her over the edge into rapture. She heard Devon roar, and his cock jerked in her ass as he filled her with his seed. Four more thrusts and Greg followed, roaring his own release as he pumped her full of semen.

Keira collapsed onto Greg's chest and clung to him as he wrapped his arms around her body. She closed her eyes and let her breathing slow until she was no longer panting. She moaned as Devon eased his cock from her ass, and then she felt him and Jake get off the bed. She was too tired and satiated to open her eyes to see what they were doing.

Greg pulled his cock from her pussy and lay down with her on the bed, and she didn't protest when she felt Devon and Jake cleaning her up with warm washcloths or when they gently patted her dry with a towel. She snuggled into Greg's chest and drifted on a soft cloud of love and protection.

She was nervous about her first shift, but knew with her mates by her side she had nothing to worry about. She would know what her men went through each time they changed and was excited to experience what is was like to be a wolf.

Chapter Fifteen

Keira stood at the edge of the clearing amongst the trees at the far end of the gardens. She was standing in a silk robe and nothing else, with her mates surrounding her. She was full of tension and nervousness, but tried to circumvent her anxiety by breathing in through her nose and out of her mouth, evenly and deeply. Her mates were touching her, rubbing their hands up and down her back and arms, trying to help keep her calm. Her skin was itching, and she had that feeling of something crawling under her skin, trying to get out.

She saw the air around Jonah shimmer and then heard the cracking and popping sounds his bones made as his body began to contort and reform. The other members of the pack followed suit until she was surrounded by wolves. Hands were on the belt of her robe, and then it was removed from her body. She felt goose bumps form on her skin, but it wasn't because she was cold. She looked up into Greg's face when he tipped her chin up with a gentle finger beneath her chin.

"Look into my eyes and let your human body fall away, baby. Keep your eyes on me. You have nothing to fear. You know we'll keep you safe," Greg said.

Keira looked deeply into Greg's eyes and felt herself drowning in their depths. She felt the moon calling to her and let her body relax as she breathed in the night air. She felt a deep ache in her bones, but it wasn't too uncomfortable or painful. She felt her body contorting, her muscles rippling beneath her skin, and her bones contracting. She looked down at her arm and saw fur sprouting along her limbs. She fell to the ground, panting as her body twisted and reshaped. When the ache was gone, she looked down and saw she was standing on paws. She looked up at her mates and stared at them in their wolf form. They were so powerful and beautiful. Even in this form they towered over her. She looked up at the moon and couldn't prevent the animal instinct of calling out with joy as the warmth she felt from the moon bathed her in its light. The echoing sounds of other wolves howling with joy filled her up with love and acceptance. She turned away from her mates and took off running.

The feel of the breeze through her fur was like having fingers threading gently through her hair. She could feel the strength of her muscles rippling as she jumped over fallen limbs and skirted around tree trunks. She had never felt so free before. She heard the sound of prey rustling in the bushes in the distance and changed direction to give chase. She played and frolicked, her mates at her sides and heels as she ran, free of her human body for the first time in her life. She was amazed at her agile four paws. Her sight was so clear, as if it were the middle of the day, and her hearing was so acute she could hear Michelle talking to the housekeeper Angela back in the kitchen.

Keira stumbled when Greg nudged her into Devon, and she looked over at him with a grin. She could see the heated stare he was giving her and took off, not wanting to give in to her mate too easily. She could hear the sounds of the other wolves chasing small prey and yipping with joy when they caught their snack. She smelled the blood as they devoured their kill and felt her mouth pool with saliva, but she had no intention of killing for the sake of it. She wasn't hungry since she'd just enjoyed a large dinner.

Keira ducked her head and nudged her shoulder into Jake's side, goading him, and then she turned and took off in the opposite direction. She could hear her three mates' paws landing so close to her flanks and put on another burst of speed. Her powerful muscles responded, and she leapt over another fallen log. She heard the sound of water in the distance and changed direction yet again. The sight of the pool of water and the waterfall feeding it entranced her. She stopped and took a drink then looked up at the kaleidoscope of colors caused by the moonlight through the small droplets of water. She had never seen anything so beautiful in her life. She looked over at Greg when he nudged her flank with his snout. His eyes were no longer brown but glowing at her with need. She looked at Jake and Devon to see them in the same condition.

She felt warmth travel to her genitals and turned her back to her mates, crouched low on all fours, and lifted her tail. Her mates didn't need to be told twice. Jake was on her first and he fucked her hard and deep. She got pleasure from the act but didn't climax. She didn't care. She felt taken over by her wolf mates and let them have their way. Jake threw his head back and howled as he filled her with his seed. He moved out of the way, and Devon was on her next. She pushed her ass back at him and growled with desire as he slid his cock in and out of her cunt. He finished quickly with a howl and moved over for Greg.

Greg covered her with his whole body, grasping her scruff in his teeth in a show of dominance which had her quivering with desire beneath him. He slammed in and out of her so hard she had to dig her claws into the soft ground for purchase. He removed his mouth from her scruff and bit down on her shoulder where he had marked her before. She felt her wolf body fill with joy and howled along with Greg as he emptied himself into her body. He withdrew his cock and nuzzled up close to her side. Jake and Devon crawled in close, resting their heads on her back and rump as she closed her eyes, savoring the exquisite moment of belonging to her mates and being able to run along with them.

She must have drifted off for a while, because her mates nudged her and she saw the moon was beginning to lower in the sky. She followed her wolf mates back to the edge of the clearing and knew it was time to change back. She watched as her mates changed from wolf to man. The sight of their naked bodies revved up her libido. She was just about to change back, but Greg's voice stopped her.

"Wait baby, let us look at you. You are gorgeous, Keira. Your coat is a light-gold color and you have light-brown-and-red highlights just like your hair," Greg stated as he ran his fingers through her fur. "Your coat is so soft and silky, and your scent is driving me crazy. Look into my eyes, Keira. See in your mind what you look like in the mirror and let your wolf fall away. That's it, baby. God, I love you."

"I love you, too. I love all of you, so damn much," Keira said when she was once more standing on two legs. She slid her arms into the robe Jake held for her and then squealed with surprise as he swept her off her feet. She felt the tip of his hard cock brushing against her silk-covered ass. She was so glad her mates seemed to be in tune with her. She was so damn horny she wanted to jump their bones out here in the open and didn't care if anyone could see.

Keira nuzzled her nose against Jake's neck and then licked and nibbled her way up to his ear. She took his lobe between her teeth and nipped him. She licked back down over his neck and inhaled his scent at the joint of his neck and shoulder. She had the urge to bite him there and claim him, but pushed it aside. He practically ran with her through the house and up the stairs to their suite of rooms.

There was a hot bath already drawn with a plate of cheeses and fruit as well as a bottle of champagne and glasses. She reached for the note she saw under the bottle when Jake let her feet down to the floor.

Welcome to the pack, sister. Enjoy. Jonah, Mikhail, and Brock.

"Aw, that's so nice," Keira breathed.

"It's their way of thanking you for saving their mate and unborn pup, baby," Greg said from behind her.

"But they've already thanked me," Keira replied.

"I don't think they'll ever stop, sweetness," Devon rumbled in her ear as he removed her robe.

Greg picked her up and stepped into the tub. He sat with her on his lap, wrapped in his body and love as she watched Jake pour champagne and Devon pick tidbits of food from the platter to feed her. In between sips and nibbles her men washed her from head to foot, and she let them. She loved that they liked to take care of her, and she knew if she wasn't careful she was going to get used to her men spoiling her. She wiggled her ass in Greg's lap and sighed with contentment as she sipped champagne.

"Are you ready for some more loving, baby?" Greg whispered in her ear.

"I thought you'd never ask," Keira replied.

Keira watched Devon stand up and get out of the large tub. He dried off and then held out a clean towel for her. Greg helped her to stand, and Jake steadied her as she stepped from the tub. She was wrapped in the large towel, and Devon began to pat her dry. She turned her head when she heard Jake and Greg get out of the tub and let her eyes wander the length of their naked bodies, then turned back to Devon and gave him the once-over. She grinned and offered Devon a saucy wink and sauntered out of the bathroom with an extra sway of her hips. The growls that followed had her laughing, which changed to squealing as she flew through the air and landed with a bounce on the soft mattress.

They were on her in an instant.

Jake pushed her legs apart and devoured her slick folds with his mouth. He pushed two fingers into her wet cunt and pumped them in and out of her body, going faster and deeper every time. He licked over her clit and then sucked the sensitive, engorged nub in between his lips. He swiped it with his tongue again and again and again.

Keira bucked her hips up into his mouth, needing a firmer contact on her clit, but Jake only chuckled and held her hips down. He teased and ate at her until she was on the edge of climax. When she thought she was about to go over, Jake pulled his mouth and hands away from her body.

Keira looked over at Greg then Devon and saw the sexy smiles on their faces. She reached up as Devon leaned down, and he slanted his mouth over hers. She opened up to him when she felt his tongue slide along her lips and sucked his muscle into her mouth. She moaned and twirled hers over his.

She felt the crown of Jake's cock at her pussy entrance and restrained herself just in time. She knew if she had pushed her hips at him, he would have held her down and made her wait a bit longer to feel his cock sliding into her cunt. She mewled as she felt the head of his dick push through her elastic flesh and Jake buried himself in her sheath to the hilt. She bucked up, trying to get him to move, but he gripped her hips and held her still. She opened her eyes and reached for Jake as he swept her up into his arms and held her tight against his body.

Keira felt warm breath on the sensitive skin of her ass and looked over her shoulder just as Greg licked around her asshole with his tongue. She moaned at the exquisite, darkly erotic act, but lifted her ass for more. When she was nice and wet, Greg moved his mouth away from her dark pucker and replaced his tongue with cool, lubed fingers. He pushed those fingers into her ass, thrusting them in and out while he spread his fingers wide, stretching her. She moaned when he withdrew his fingers and presented her ass to him as he began to push his hard cock into her anus. She pushed back against him and sobbed as he slid into her tight canal until his balls were on her flesh.

Keira turned her head, searching for Devon, and when his cock slid across her lips, she opened wide and sucked him down. She drew on him hard then bobbed her head up and down the length of his dick. The moan she gave as Jake and Greg began to fuck her ass and pussy was muffled by Devon's big rod.

Her mates took turns gliding their dicks in and out of her two holes, one retreating while the other advanced. She was never once empty of cock as her mates fucked her. Her mouth, ass, and pussy were filled to capacity with each thrust of her men's hips. The sensational pleasure was so much more now that she was a werewolf.

She could feel them in her blood, and she didn't ever want them to stop.

Keira felt the liquid ache deep in her womb, and the warm tingles permeating her lower body burned hotter. She sucked and licked on Devon as Greg and Jake shuttled their cocks in and out of her holes. The coils gathered tighter than they had ever been before, and she didn't know if she would survive the pleasure. She felt Devon's cock expand and slid him down her throat, swallowing around the head of his dick. He roared as he spewed his load down her throat. She gulped down his seed, not wanting to waste a single drop. He withdrew his cock from her mouth after the last shudder rippled through his body, and she threw her head back, screaming as he rubbed on her clit. Her pelvic-floor muscles clamped down on the two cocks in her ass and cunt, and she felt Jake's and Greg's rods jerk and fill her with their essence. She felt her pussy's liquid release and continued to cry out until the last spasm died a natural death.

Keira slumped against Greg and didn't protest when her mates cleaned her up and tucked her into bed between them. Greg, Jake, and Devon each leaned in close to her and sniffed at her neck. They moved away and howled with joy. *What was up with that?*

Epilogue

Keira had told her mates last night that she intended to sell off her parents' house. She didn't need it because there was no way in hell she was leaving her mates' sides. She loved that she was surrounded by so many pack members, whom she now considered her family. She was going to give the proceeds of the house to charity.

She still had more than enough money from her trust fund. She wouldn't have to work another day in her life if she didn't want to, but she still wanted to work because she hated being bored and liked to pull her weight. The police had told her mates that all of David's employers had been rounded up and incarcerated. Apparently her brother had kept records of names and transactions on a spreadsheet on his PC which had led the law to the other perpetrators. She was glad she wouldn't have to worry about anyone else coming after her.

Keira walked into the dining room where her mates waited for her. It was the night after her first change, and she was famished. She took her seat between Greg and Jake and saw them staring at her with wonder and heat in their eyes. She looked around when she realized everyone was quiet and saw all the men sniffing the air and looking at her.

"What? I had a shower," Keira stated grumpily, crossing her arms over her chest in defense.

The howls and catcalls thundering through the room hurt her ears. She looked around when she saw the men closest to her mates slapping them on the back, congratulating them. *What the hell?*

Greg leaned in close to Keira and sniffed her neck, the same as he and his brothers had done last night. She leaned into him and gave him access without thinking about everyone watching them.

"You smell delicious, mate," Greg rumbled out

"Greg, what are you doing? Jake, stop that. Devon, oh for crying out loud," Keira said as she stood and moved back from her mates. "One of you better tell me what the hell is going on before I start screaming."

"You are screaming, baby," Greg replied with grin as he stalked toward her like a predator hunting prey.

"Stay where you are," Keira said, holding her hand palm up to halt his progress.

"You're breeding, Keira," Jake stated with deep emotion, as he moved toward her from her other side.

"I am not," Keira replied. "Look, I am so hungry I could eat a whole cow raw, now let me sit down and eat my breakfast before I lose my temper."

"Are you feeling a bit grouchy, sweetness?" Devon asked from near Greg.

"Yeah, and the cause has three names, Greg, Jake, and Devon. Now back off," Keira stated with emphasis and stopped with bewilderment when she heard her own voice sounding deeper than usual.

"Oh my," Keira said and stumbled over to her chair and collapsed. "I am pregnant, otherwise I wouldn't be craving raw meat. It's all your fault," she grumbled and burst into tears. Her mates crowded around her and tried to soothe and comfort her.

"Baby, why are you crying? I thought you'd be happy to have our pup," Greg asked with concern.

Keira reached up and touched the palm of her hand against his cheek and wailed. "I am happy."

"Well, that's all right then. Let me get you some food, baby," Greg said.

"Do you want some milk, honey?" Jake asked.

"How about some herbal tea, sweetness?" Devon asked.

Oh boy, Keira thought and mentally rolled her eyes. It was going to be hard keeping her mates from driving her crazy. *Maybe I should drive them crazy first?* Keira burst out laughing at the thought. Her three men just gave her silly grins and kept pushing food and drink at her, and she wouldn't have had it any other way. She loved them just the way they were.

THE END

WWW.BECCAVAN-EROTICROMANCE.COM

ABOUT THE AUTHOR

My name is Becca Van. I live in Australia with my wonderful hubby of many years, as well as my two children.

I read my first romance at the age of thirteen, which I found in the school library, and haven't stopped reading them since. It is so wonderful to know that love is still alive and strong when there seems to be so much conflict in the world.

I dreamed of writing my own book one day but unfortunately, didn't follow my dream for many years. But once I started I knew writing was what I wanted to continue doing.

I love to escape from the world and curl up with a good romance, to see how the characters unfold and conflict is dealt with. I have read many books and love all facets of the romance genre, from historical to erotic romance. I am a sucker for a happy ending.

Also by Becca Van

Ménage Everlasting: Pack Law 1: *Set Me Free*
Ménage Everlasting: Pack Law 3: *Mate for Three*
Ménage Everlasting: Terra-form 1: *Alpha Panthers*
Ménage Everlasting: Terra-form 2: *Taming Olivia*
Ménage Everlasting: Terra-form 3: *Keeley's Opposition*

For all other titles, please visit
www.bookstrand.com/becca-van

Siren Publishing, Inc.
www.SirenPublishing.com

CPSIA information can be obtained at www.ICGtesting.com
Printed in the USA
BVOW021227270513

321720BV00009B/242/P

9 781622 410880